T0354567

THE CHASM

THE CHASM

Prativa Chakraborty

PARTRIDGE
A Penguin Random House Company

To order additional copies of this book, contact
Partridge India
000 800 10062 62
www.partridgepublishing.com/india
orders.india@partridgepublishing.com

For Ma and Baba

1905

CALCUTTA, INDIA

"We've got to do something, Viceroy", said Mark as he paced up and down clad in his red suit. The roar of protests was being obstructed by the thick glass of the window and only angry people could be seen spitting out their rage in the scorching heat outside.

"Patience, Mark. We need to look before we leap. Every step will be taken into account", Said the grave viceroy who sat pondering at his desk.

"Bengal has been too good to us Mark, don't you think? But I smell the brewing of something underneath, though I have no complaints against them as long as it causes no harm to the Empire."

"Perhaps you are endowed with too much subtlety, Sir to deal with them but with such grace."

Mark was not sure if the Viceroy had understood his remark, for the next few lines uttered by the grave man took him by absolute amazement. "Moreover I also have to look after the people's needs here. Could you bring me that file from there? I think there's a village in the south of Bengal as they say that is going through a famine. Call for a meeting. We have to discuss matters", he had said, like Mark had not spoken at all.

The Viceroy looked out of the window as he spoke. He sighed as his eyes fell on the barren dried up land that lay ahead where the helpless and poor Indians waited with some last hopes from the foreigners. People had forgotten how long they were being ruled over so brutally by the invincible East India Company. Despair never left their side since scores of years now. Futile efforts had been made to retrieve the lost freedom and peace. Lord Curzon was not totally unaffected by the poor people's helpless yet propitious temperament but some very coherent policies rendered his empathy (even if it was very little) void.

Hardly had the Viceroy realized that Mark had left the room some minutes ago while he sat quietly embracing solitude. The emptiness in his eyes reflected his great grandfather's portrait as he stared at it aimlessly. Unknowingly he was imitating it with his arms folded with a curious frown and his hair were the same golden locks that rested carelessly on his shoulders. Thoughts, which had disappeared somewhere between the blankness and tiredness were beginning to return. The political scenario hadn't been quite impressive during these times. They had to act immediately or lose everything. Mark had been right. Lord Curzon groped for his glasses so that he could read the complaints on the file properly.

He had to do something to strengthen British power more and more, not that he meant any harm to the Indians either. Somewhere deep within he too did not go unabashed of the cruelty and the injustice that the people were going through, here in India, but all that was shrouded beneath the thick invincible layer of vanity of the Royal blood.

As he walked through the serene dim aisle with the file in his hands he rehearsed his speech that he had prepared to address the parley of men waiting for him at the conference room.

As soon as he entered, everybody stood up.

"Good morning and Please take your seats gentlemen." He knew what he had to say but what he didn't know was how he would start. After a minute's silence he finally spoke "as we know we are all gathered here to discuss about the famine—

The room filled with instant murmurs when Lord Curzon Cleared his throat aloud and continued stressing on every word he spoke, "AND ABOUT THE POLITICAL TROUBLES THAT WE ARE FACING AT THIS TIME. Gentlemen I understand the predicament, and I am trying hard to get us all out of this situation but not without your help and cooperation. I hope that you understand that the misery of the people here is having adverse affects on our political situation. Everything at this moment is interrelated. We cannot neglect any minor matter right now." Everybody straightened up as if now they were ready to hear what the Viceroy had to say.

A stout middle aged man sitting right beside Curzon raised his short finger in the air.

"Mr. Hopkins," said Curzon with his strong voice, "I assume you have something to share with us."

"I was wondering if a pipe could be connected to the huge water tank that supplies water to us, that is a pipe leading to the village in question and a timely water supply for the irrigation—"

His opinion was broken by a room full of commotion along with some mockery about the concern that the man showed for the host country.

Lord Curzon wore a smile while the chaos was arrested by him asking his men to settle down, "Gentlemen I need you to stop behaving like the uncivilized gathered out there. Can we maintain decorum please? And Mr. Hopkins, I mean no offense here but the Empire cannot afford to compromise with its luxuries to provide the villagers with anything. Moreover they are used to seeing their places rife with poverty all their life. They work really hard; do not defy their abilities to improvise with their strategies. They can produce water if they want to. All we need to do is keep them on our side."

It wasn't long before another argument started that left the main topic untouched and everybody tried to make their point noticed which was more likely to be for their personal benefit.

The meeting carried on for about one and a half hour without any proper decision and so it was called off until sometime someone cropped with an appropriate solution. Everyone rose from their seats to leave the hall when the Viceroy asked his secretary, Mark to stay back. When everybody had disappeared he finally spoke to Mark, "I was wondering if you got any news from Addison, Mark—

The rest of his words were drowned into the sounds of furniture being dragged somewhere upstairs.

Mark replied in great suspicion if that was an appropriate reply to the question, "Uh—Sir he is supposed to be arriving tonight but I'm afraid we have not received any confirmation from Sir Addison yet" and was relieved to discover that his guess was right.

"Oh that kid will never change. As far as I conceive he is planning for a surprise visit. You know how much I hate that Mark; I hate to keep the mansion undecorated when my only son's visiting my empire for the first time in his life."

A short yet very pretty girl came running from somewhere behind and grabbed Lord Curzon with joy causing him to trip and take support at the nearest furniture. "Good Morning daddy!" she beamed.

"Emma how many times do I have to tell you that you've grown up now, you're sixteen darling, it is high time you stopped being so juvenile anymore."

She didn't seem to pay heed to what had just been said and letting go of her father spoke to Mark instead, "Do you know anything about Addie's arrival? Didn't he say that he'd be reaching tonight in one of his letters?"

"I am not sure about it Ma'am, we didn't receive any letter from him of late," said Mark.

"Oh if I know him well he'll give a surprise visit in a day two or maybe he could also show up tonight." Emma was too excited to speak and doing her little jig said to her father, "I'm so happy daddy! Addie's goin' to come home finally. I'll go and tell Mohar about the good news." She ran back to her room.

Lord Curzon looked out of the window and sighed at the sight. The fiery weather outside had maimed the aggressiveness of the crowd and the helpless villagers sat all dreary still not giving up on their demands.

"Ramdas" he called out loud.

A withered old man wearing a turban came hopping in "Ji sahib" he said bowing down humbly to his master.

"Explain them that we are looking after the matter of their demands and that we will soon come to a solution. They do not have to sit around here every day. I don't want to see that crowd from tomorrow. Am I crystal clear Ramdas?"

"Ji Sahib. I'll convince them."

Lord Curzon stood looking out of the window as he saw the old man walking in haste towards the mob that sat expectantly wishing for a change to take place. He felt sorry for while for those people who had been baked under the sun and then changed his mind, while he realized that these uneducated ruffians deserve what they are getting.

After a very long persuasion the crowd was sent away with new hopes in their hearts. Lord Curzon heard the screeching sound of the huge gates being closed.

CHAPTER 1

Rabindranath Mukherjee, a handsome, honest and rich gentleman with a happy family of four children and a beautiful wife couldn't have asked anything more for himself in these twenty five years of his marital life. Apart from being a very amiable and responsible husband he was also a very affectionate father. Unlike other people in the society he was always of the impression that he was very lucky to have a daughter in the family who was perhaps his lucky charm; not that he loved his sons any less. One particular thing he was relieved about was that in spite of a foreign rule in the country he and his family were enjoying a very good social status and a peaceful life and he never forgot to thank god for that at least twice every day.

After graduating from law school with extraordinary marks Rabin had started practicing very early. Money had always somehow made its way into the house since then. He first met his wife only on their wedding night and luckily he found her to be very pretty and quite innocent. Apparently she was only fourteen then and eleven years younger than her husband.

Ratna Mukherjee had done her job quite well all these years. Though before the marriage she was skeptical about getting hitched to a person who was eleven years older than her and she wouldn't deny the fact that there was a rebellion growing inside her to protest against this; but she was considerate enough to improvise because a girl speaking against her parents' wishes was the biggest felony she would ever commit. Gradually she became familiar to all adjustments she had to make with her life. One golden rule that she had learned that had given her a happy life was keeping quiet when others in the family are speaking, especially some elder or her husband. Nobody liked a woman putting forth her opinion because it was believed to be inherent in women that they are dumb and can show their wisdom only by staying grave and maintaining their silence. Ratna respected her husband and never went against his wishes.

The first night they made love is the night she will remember forever. Apparently it was not any of her best memories. She swore she knew nothing of that sort would happen because she had no idea what making love meant; she respected her husband and according to her, stripping shamelessly in front of her was not at all a human-like thing to do for such a grown up man. It was only later on that she realized that only grown up men did such things with their wives but the reason was unknown to her because pleasure was something she had not yet come across while having sex, so she assumed that this was the only way they could have children and so she had to do it whether or not she approved of it was irrelevant.

Rabin was then going through the happiest phase of his life. His new bride couldn't have been better. She was beautiful, obedient and cooked very delicious food. Apart from that he was rich. Sometimes he could also say that other men envied him which he enjoyed a lot.

Ratna was also satisfied with what she had got. She was very grateful to her husband for the recognition that she had got in the society. People respected her because she was the wife of one of the most successful lawyers in town and also lived in one of the biggest bungalows. Piousness was another quality that she possessed. She would fast quite often for her husband's undaunted success which never went in vain.

She was sixteen when she had her first child. It had left her all emaciated. But the joyous celebrations all around had compelled her to stay fit. Her first child was a boy and people all around had congratulated her whole heartedly. "We were scared you might give birth to a girl, but since you pray with such purity you were blessed with a boy Ratan", her near and dear ones had said. Ratna didn't quite like it but she preferred to stick to her golden rule.

Rabin was very happy for his first son but he had no grudges against a girl either. Unlike others he believed that a girl was necessary in the house because a girl child was considered to be the goddess of wealth.

Ratan was twenty when she learned that she was pregnant again. She gave birth to a boy again. It called for a second celebration in the town. The hostess was still recovering yet she didn't show a bit on her countenance. Ditto events happened again when she gave birth to her third son two years later.

Two years later Rabin's wishes were fulfilled and Ratan gave birth to a girl. They also named her Mohar which meant precious gems. The couple was preparing for a similar celebration when they realized that not half of their friends and relatives had turned up. Perhaps the ones who had come were quite conspicuously pretending to be blissful. The couple had kept quiet lest their reputation in the society would be hampered.

Yet among their guests there was a woman who was overwhelmed with joy for Mohar's birth. She was Mrs. Kamala Chatterjee, the woman who lived next door. Ratna and Kamala had known each other since Ratna's marriage. Ratna loved her the moment she met her. Ever since then the two of them had been there for each other through thick and thin like soul mates. The stout round eyed woman was sometimes jealous of beautiful Ratna but that was temporary.

When Mohar was five Kamala had confided into Ratna about her secret wishes, "I was wondering, my dear Ratan, wouldn't it be wonderful if your Mohar got married to my Vikram?"

All the excitement during Mohar's birth had fallen into place now. Ratna couldn't deny that Vikarm had already started looking really good and also was very smart and intelligent, though he was only 12 and it was too early to judge.

"Yeah Kamala di", she said "I think that'll be great. The two of them will get to know each other from their childhood days too."

When Rabin returned from office that night, Ratna announced the good news in the family at the dinner table. The news was sudden and quick yet not totally unexpected. The family next door was rich and maintained a status in the society; moreover Rabin adored the boy so he was happy with his wife's decision. That was the first decision she had ever taken in the family and Rabin felt proud of her.

Rabin never discriminated among his children. Though Ratna was of the opinion that a girl didn't have much to do with education but Rabin thought differently. He knew its worth. So all the siblings including Mohar, went to the International School. The boys were just like their father and also interested in law. But the girl had her mother's long forgotten (or may be suppressed would be an appropriate word) rebellion attitude. Despite her unusual attitude Mohar she was her father's favourite. She learned music and dance and also excelled in both of them and considered herself to be lucky that she didn't have to face any such situations in her life when she would have to go against her father's wishes.

CHAPTER 2

LONDON 1905

The farewell speech was as boring as ever but the only thing that kept him from passing out was Mrs. Wesley, the Political Science head mistress. She had an aura of freshness hovering about her and her glamorous yet a bit tanned skin seemed to attract Addison Albert Curzon and felt helpless when he couldn't take his eyes off her. George who could feel the awkwardness of the situation sitting beside Addie nudged him again and again trying his best to distract and mumbled exasperatedly, "Addie! What are you doin'??" Addison would stop ogling at her for a moment and sit straight upright with his tall and lanky figure but before he could fathom what was going on in the hall he would return to square one.

The programme carried on till two hours and Addison utilized every bit of it fantasizing about his dream woman. There was something unusual about her. He couldn't calculate if it was out of the regular tan or her thin outline or her big yet very curvy and pretty eyes or was it just like the other boys said; her "voluptuous breasts" that kept him enchanted every time she showed up. When he came back to his senses he found his friend shaking him and yelling, "Addie!! The speech is over! Get up and let's leave."

Addison looked utterly bewildered at him and replied, "Where are the others? Where did she go?"

George sighed, "What is she? A witch? How does she do that?"

George and Addison had been roommates ever since they started studying law in Harvard. They were the best of friends and never missed any moment in these five years when they could have fun. The game attracted them a lot. One thing that was common in both the boys was that they were outstanding athletes and showed their keen interest in sports very conspicuously. Each of the two was a captain of two rival teams that played cricket within the university. Though the game never gave rise to any vendetta between the two best buddies they knew how to take the opposition sportingly, and tackled with their trivial strives with an extreme sportsmanship spirit.

The room was no unusual place but the typical dwelling house of two rough men who liked to keep their area smelling of cricket with helmets hanging neatly on the wall and posters of their favourite players pasted all over the wall. There were two beds at two corners of the room which was cleaned everyday by Mrs. Scrooge and in between were their wardrobes. Once during an argument Addison had punched angrily on the wardrobe that had created a dent on it. After the boys had reconciled they laughed about the damage they had made and to hide it from the maid they had stuck a picture of a local lady singer who was a heartthrob in the town. The maid would look at it with utter jealousy.

Addie had just stepped out of the bathroom when the fat and ugly woman knocked on the door.

"Room cleaning", she said in her usual whining tone.

George who was busy with something and nearer to the door opened it for her not noticing the fact that Addie had not yet dressed himself up. The maid was a middle aged single woman, walked in with her broom and looked quite satisfied as she witnessed a young boy with his towel wrapped around his waist. She turned pink as she ran her eyes through his tall and lanky figure as water trickled from his chin to his waist line. Addie stood teasing the lady's position when he winked at his friend and smiling to himself.

"I think I should come back later." She said hesitating to look at him directly on his face.

"Oh no, Mrs. Bennet it's perfectly fine. Please continue with your work." Addison enjoyed the attention while his friend sat on his bed trying hard to stop himself from exploding out with laughter.

An envelope just showed from under the bed as she swept the room. Addison picked it up curiously and was aghast to see that it was the letter he had written to his father about his arrival in India the next week.

He leapt with strides traverse the room and knocked his friend his head.

"Ouch!" he said rubbing his head, "what are you doin'?"

"What's this?" Addison held the letter up in the air, staring at his friend with deadly eyes.

"Oh no! Man I'm sorry I just forgot about your letter." George gave him apologetic looks through his round glasses as innocence tried its best to hide the guilt of sheer negligence.

"George I trusted you with one thing and you just let your carelessness prove me wrong!" he shouted angrily. "This letter" he said as he showed him the letter again and again "was to inform my family that I will be reaching India by next week and now they have no idea whenever I am arriving!"

George didn't want to argue this time because he knew that he was wrong this time and there was no way of exonerating himself from this situation. He sat looking genuinely sorry for what he had done.

"Now say something." Said Addison who had least expected his best friend to keep quiet in a situation like this when suddenly it dawned on him that the boy who had always fought with him even when he knew that he was wrong was now keeping quiet and apologizing to his best friend which had never been a cliché before.

He dropped the letter on his bed and move closer to George yet not sitting on his bed lest he would break down if by any chance George hugged him, which was quite obvious by his disposition. George sat quietly on the bed with his head drooped down contemplating to himself.

"I'll miss you buddy", he murmured.

"I'll miss you too", Addison replied realizing the truth in his statement.

He bucked up courage and sat down beside George on his bed. The warmth and hysteria of the moment added to the boys' emotional sadness about the separation. No sooner had Addison put an arm across George's shoulder than he turned around and hugged him tightly.

"I did it on purpose", he confessed, "I wanted your leave to be delayed."

Addison understood the feeling and maintained his silence feeling the moist in his eyes. When the two boys separated Addie said, "It's ok George, I understand, but my departure cannot be delayed any further. I'm afraid

I will have to leave tomorrow. My family is waiting eagerly for my arrival."

"Yeah, uh, no, I'm alright. I understand that you're going cannot be delayed. It's ok. It's just that everything happened so fast that I didn't realize when we grew up and it was time to say good bye already." Addison was not quite surprised at how miserable George looked 'cause he felt the same.

He rose from the bed and advanced towards his wardrobe and casually spoke to his best friend trying to seem normal, "now get up and give me a hand, I need help with my packing."

The two best friends sat talking and that the same time Addison rummaged all his possessions in his bag and a huge suitcase that he was worried about being questioned at the airport for being too heavy.

CHAPTER 3

KOLKATA 1905

Mohar Mukherjee would observe the proprieties of the neighbourhood yet loath to adapt to its preening and prancing attitude. She would consider herself to be a fish out of water in this typical society of the twentieth century. Her feelings were often subdued by the incessant attempts of her mother but it was not long before when she returned to square one. Fifteen years did not seem to be susceptible enough to make an ideal woman out of a juvenile.

The rich spoilt beloved sister of three brothers returned all exhausted late in the evening when the sun had set already. "You! ma'am! This is a serious breach of the rules of social conduct!", Mrs. Mukherjee yelled angrily at her prodigal daughter. "Mother—", her eldest brother had started when their mother raised her right hand towards him which he fathomed was a gesture to ask him to shut up. "No more defending your sister, Shohom!", she spat exasperatedly.

"But she was with us mother. What's wrong in a little girl playing with her brothers?"

"Mohar is no more a 'little' girl Shohom. Is she? She is sixteen already and she ought to be married in a year or two. And who would possibly marry a girl who still likes hopping about with boys and wearing these", she looked at what she was wearing and then shaking her head in disapproval said, "I don't know what and playing cricket with those English!"

"This is a beautiful dress mother! And what's wrong with it? Emma gifted it to me last summer", she examined the frills and stitches in her frock that her English best friend had given her.

"Now, THAT, has sabotaged your social behavior Mohar. You must not mix with the English so much. And that goes to you too", she said looking sternly at her sons, who had already started devouring the fruits from the table. Mohar would not stop being friends with Emma despite her mother's futile attempts to stop her from going around with the girl. "I'll have to talk to your father about this."

She mumbled something to herself angrily and stormed out of the room.

A gusty wind was blowing outside. Servants and maids were running all over the mansion to close all doors and windows. Upstairs in her room at one corner the distracting creaking sounds of the swinging chandeliers penetrated through the depth of her thoughts. Her father had his own identity and people looked up to him in the society. Mohar wanted to be like her father. Vanity and independence was the cloth she was cut from. She wanted to pursue law like her brothers and father. But somewhere deep down her conscience she dreaded her mother's rage of insinuation about her ambition. Thoughts pouring in and out of her mind left her staring at nothing but the black window glass.

The moving silhouettes on the dark road outside drew her attention suddenly. A speeding carriage had in the midst of this vexed night accidentally dropped its tailboard somewhere. The noise added to the chafing weather. A tall man descended from the carriage grabbing his hat trying to shun the dust away. Someone knocked on the door when Mrs. Mukherjee was laying the table for dinner. "Mohar", she called out, "Must be your father. Could you open the door darling?" She ran down the stairs hastily with strides towards the door. The bottom of her dress brushed all over the floor. She knew it wasn't her father. A dusty dry wave of cold air smacked on her face as soon as she opened the door and though it had blinded her she stole a glance from the corner of her eye. A very young and handsome man stood at the door. She realized that he was English and not from the neighbourhood.

Before he could say anything she twirled around foolishly rubbing her eyes and said to her mother, "There's a man at the door I know not of."

Two of her brothers, Kali and Shivu appeared from behind her mother to attend the man. "May I help you?", said Kali.

"Um. Uh my carriage seems to have broken down in the middle of the road. I was wondering would you mind if I took shelter at your place while men are trying to fix it up as it is quite an unpleasant weather outside", the man hesitated but spoke without breathing as if he was scared of denial.

"Oh yes of course. Come in" Kali extended his hand greeting the stranger in. "I'm Kali and this is my brother Shivu."

"Hello. I am Addison from London" the word *London* echoed vanity inevitably.

While Shivu took the lad's coat Mohar stood admiring his gentleman-like manners though not showing any of her admiration on her countenance.

"Please do take a seat, sir", Shivu spoke.

Someone knocked on door while they talked. Kali ran to open the door for his father. Instead, a hooded figure stood with a lamp in his right hand. He had to speak out loud because of the wind. "Rabindranath babu has sent a message for his family. He has some very important errand to complete and so he won't return home tonight." The mask of the untidy shawl protected the face from the dust that was attacking its prey. Before anyone could question any further the man turned around and limped away like he was in a great hurry.

A whirl of wind rushed into the house and before the doors could be shut again the chandelier swung out of control. Hardly had anyone noticed the hook when it unfastened itself and gravity had done its work better than any other instance before. The bunch of heavy glass illuminations descended with a crash shattering into numerous pieces. Disastrous as it was, the catastrophic momentum of the whole scenario had earned all the attention concealing an earnest endeavor to save someone's life successfully at one interesting corner of the hall.

Mohar who was standing just below the huge showy lights, stood witnessing jeopardy speeding helplessly towards her when Addison had from her side pulled her by the arm and saved her from this accident. With everyone else traverse the room behind the fallen chandelier the two of them were left alone at one dimly illuminated corner. The two souls connected with their bodies closest to each other. Her eyes shone with a conspicuous merriment with a pair of masculine arms circling her while she stood, thanking the almighty ironically for her safety. Moments after the fall of the gigantic light he stood holding her unwilling to let go. Not that either of them wanted to. Astonishingly, her tanned fairness and polite eyes dictated his meditations. Amidst the involvement of different thoughts from different borders with an undying curiosity to unveil the secrets into the depths of their eyes revealed the raw unwillingness to be interrupted.

Yet from a distance on the realization of their little girl's absence came a concerned brother's voice "Mohar? Mr. Addison? Are you alright?"

The distraction was sudden and the feelings had disappeared instantly like it had been a dream that only left some mere hangovers.

"We are—uh—we are fine Mr. Kali." The arms loosened and let go of the possession that had been acquired for a brief yet one of the most cherished moments of one's life.

"Dada I'm ok." Mohar walked away quickly and embraced reality holding her brother. Mrs. Mukherjee seemed to have smelled a rat already but Mohar ignored her suspicious glares.

The servants were called for and in no time they had started cleaning the mess up diligently while Mrs. Mukherjee disappeared into the dark, looking rather annoyed. Some candles were brought and lightened and all this while Mohar rehearsed the last few course of events in her mind again and again ensuring herself that it wasn't a dream.

The two strangers tried not to meet each others' eyes yet stole some quick glances from the corner of the eye and smiled carefully to themselves.

The grateful brothers shook hands with Mr. Addison. "We can't thank you enough Addison for saving our sister's life," said Kali. "I think you should dine with us tonight", came a responsible request from the eldest, Shohom.

"Yes Mr. Addison we would request you to stay back for dinner on this tormented night."

The proposal was sudden but not too difficult to accept. It was something the man wanted, some more time to spend here. Yet he hesitated and then replied, "oh—uh—well I guess I would love to have dinner with you" and just then his mind had made an earnest interrogation to itself "have you ever had ethnic food before *Mr. Addison the savior?*"

The table was laid soon and the brothers ushered Mr. Collins to the dining hall. The décor was adorable with candles on the table and neat, pretty drapes all around the place. The food was served and it honestly looked quite spicy.

"Is everything alright, Mr. Addison?" Shohom enquired noticing the horrid expression on his face.

"Addie" he said.

"Sorry?" replied Shohom looking quite confused.

"Call me Addie and I'm perfectly fine. Thank you"

All inhibitions gave way to liking Indian food when Addie started eating. It was surprisingly delicious.

There was an awkward silence for the rest of the dinner. Mrs. Mukherjee was still not happy about something and the brothers were nudging each other gesturing secretly asking about their mother's discontent.

Finally Addie broke the silence when he spoke "The dinner was really good Mrs. Mukherjee. And thank you gentlemen for inviting me for dinner, I was saved from being tormented to death on this terrible night."

But before anyone could say anything there was another knock on the door. "I'll get that", said Shohom as he rose from his chair and advanced towards the door.

"Addie", he called out soon "the tailboard of your carriage has been fixed, pal. One of the men had come to inform you."

"Oh thank god", he sighed. "I was starting to worry."

They finished dinner.

"I must scoot now, pals"

"It was nice to have you for dinner tonight son", added Mrs. Mukherjee gently smiling and speaking for the first time since Addie's arrival.

"Thank you Mrs. Mukherjee and it was nice to meet you people and thank you for having me as your guest even at such a sudden moment's notice."

As he extended his hand to the brothers he quickly looked straight at Mohar and within a heart's beat looked away. But even in that small timing their eyes met causing a sudden sensation which neither of them was aware of, they just knew that the feeling was extremely pleasant yet disturbing.

The door closed behind him as soon as Addie had stepped out of the house.

No sooner did the door close that Mohar turned around and spoke "What's wrong with you mother?"

"You think I don't understand anything?", her mother retorted.

"What are you talking about?"

"About whatever was happening at that corner!" her lanky fingers were raised at the direction of the corner where Addie had held Mohar in his arms when the chandelier had crashed down.

"For god sake mother he saved my life! And I don't want to discuss on this matter with you anymore!"

Mohar ran upstairs angrily.

"What is the matter with you, mother?" Shohom asked raising his eyebrows looking quite disappointed at her accusations.

"You didn't see the two of them Shohom. I'm really concerned about this girl. I dread the day she would elope with some British."

"And why would she do that?"

"I'm her mother, I know what she is like. Who would know her better? She needs a husband soon."

"But she is too young, Ma."

"I already had my first child when I was her age. After all it is inherent in us girls to accept whatever fate has to offer us. It is essential that her make-beliefs are nipped in the bud."

"Ma, you are taking this way too far. We shouldn't rush into taking decisions. It is the girl's life. We need to ask her first."

"I don't have to *ask* anything. I'm her mother and she has to obey my orders."

"But—"

"I'm **your** mother too! And I order you not argue any further I know what's best for my children while they seem to have lost their senses! It would be best for you to go to bed now and also take your brothers with you!"

The disappointed brothers left the room helplessly, trudging upstairs with their faces drooping with disapproval. Talking back to parents was not an acceptable behavior at all but all the Mukherjee kids seemed to have inherited their mother's suppressed attitude of opposing against anything that was wrong or unjust. The mother's knowledge about this always begged her secretly to consider her kids' behavior to some extent. An invisible forgotten part of her also seemed to take a liking towards it.

CHAPTER 4

Meandering thoughts raced his mind as soon as the carriage started moving. Curiosity gave way to nervousness while Addison sat advancing towards his home wondering what his father's reaction would be on seeing his only son show up without any early notice after almost seven years. The weather was still windy and the jerks because of the uneven roads made him all the more exasperated. He started taking a dislike for the place immediately when suddenly something forced him to change his mind. Amidst the counting of all bad things he had faced the moment he landed in the country a beautiful piece of memory that he had gathered at the same time nudged the worst of his meditations making way for a tiny little twitch in his heart. He tried to ignore at first and shun away the feeling thinking it was too soon and too stupid to think like that. Evidently he couldn't help and most surprisingly without any effort his lips stretched as far as they could to the either corners of his cheeks and he looked down even in the dark carriage to hide his secret misgivings. But the sudden relief had made him inquisitive. He witnessed the timid countenance that concealed valiant pretensions as he stared with augmenting admiration at the beauty that fell into his arms that evening. Her image was soothing enough for him to forget all of his worries. He had been mesmerized by her sight. Not that she had not wanted him to; but pretended to be unaware of the aura that lingered strong enough to leave the man transfixed even in the dark. The weather outside ironically reflected his mind. Her tanned yet golden skin and round sparkling eyes was a typically different beauty that shone bright enough to capture his total attention. Her sweet voice still rang into his ears.

The carriage came to a stop with a jolt.

"Saheb", the driver called out, "we are there."

Addie was distracted from his reverie and now knew was his turn to answer some really serious questions which would be directed by his father. He was groping in his pocket for change when he heard the carriage puller say, "thank you Saheb."

He looked up all bewildered and hopped to the other side of the vehicle to see who was kind enough to pay for him. His lips parted to sigh with disbelief of what his eyes beheld. His father still looked like he had last seen him, tough and handsome, not a day older. The only barrier between the father and the son moved away monotonously, and disappeared into the dark leaving behind an awkward silence. Addie felt thankful that it was pitch black and his father couldn't see his eyes because he felt his eyes were moist with happiness. The wind had stopped but it had started drizzling now. Lord Curzon embraced his son without a word. He had a lump in his throat on finally meeting the boy after so many years. Two servants came running with umbrellas and escorted the men inside the mansion while one of the servants also carried Addie's luggage.

"Thank you", said Addie looking at the servants.

"Welcome to India, my dear son", his father finally spoke his voice shaking with a satisfactory smile on his face.

"Thank you father", said Addie as the two of them hugged each other again, this time laughing at their own blissfulness.

"Why wouldn't you inform us before showing up?" asked the concerned father.

"Oh father, where do I start from? There was a grave misunderstanding and somehow the letter about my homecoming that was supposed to be posted long before my arrival here was missed and—

"Oh-my-god! Addie!!" yelled his sister from upstairs interrupting him as Addie saw her run down the curvy staircase as swiftly as ever. Before he could balance himself properly his sister came striding over and pounced on him. But for Addie's unquestionable maneuvering abilities (just like the little incident from before) they were saved from falling down backwards and he grabbed his sister with all the love. Emma stammered happily into his ears, "Oh I have missed you so much." Addie loosened arms around her "I have missed you too Em" he said.

Emma hopped around and adorably reprimanded her father, "started questioning him already, haven't you?"

"Emma, my son has returned home after seven years! May we have some privacy please?"

"So has my brother, daddie! So, no, you may not!" she kissed her brother on the cheek as she hopped about excitedly.

"Emma", said her father, "he must be tired after such a long journey why don't you let him go for a moment."

"Dad, it's okay, I'm fine." Said Addie.

"I'll let you two have fun but tomorrow early in the morning I want you to be ready we have business to talk", said Lord Curzon quite sternly.

"Tomorrow morning he's all yours papa," promised Emma.

"Good night kids. Emma, why don't you usher him to his room and ask one of those men to carry his luggage upstairs?" suggested the grave old man.

"Consider it done, sir" giggled Emma.

"Addison, since you're tired your dinner will be served upstairs in your room."

"Uh Father, I already had dinner on my way. I was stuck because of the weather and an Indian family helped me out. They seemed quite good."

"Ah, well," His father turned around unexpectedly and without a word walked away to his room while he nodded in silence.

Emma held her brother's hand tightly and pulled him with all her strength towards the stairs.

While she escorted him to his room she kept her questioning session on.

"So who did you have dinner with Addie?" she asked instantly.

"I don't know them they are the family who live round the corner about four to five mansions from here in the next alley.

"Yeah, that's ok but didn't you ask their names?"

"Yes of course I did. I the guy said his name was uh, well do you except me to remember such weird names, Em?"

"What? No. Their names aren't that weird. They are just unique," Emma seemed to be annoyed with her brother's inappropriate comment about the people she was fond of.

Emma's unexpected comment took her brother to surprise and he teased her, "Oh this country seems to have won your heart."

Emma's closest friend, Mohar had been an Indian and the country had quite inescapably covered a place in her heart. She smiled at her brother's sudden remark and as if she did over all her cherished memories she said, "Yes Addie, this country is very beautiful, and the people here are way too innocent. I'm glad you've come home too, you'll start loving it here as well."

A sudden uninvited yet very pleasant picture of Addison's first most pleasant memory crossed his mind and he didn't doubt his sister's admiration for the place she grew up in. They finally reached to his room when Addison stopped at the door step and putting arm across his sister's shoulders smiled as he spoke, "So; we are there."

"Hmmm" said Emma realizing the situation's flexibility, "And now I'll take your leave, you must be tired. I hope you have a peaceful sleep."

"Yeah you too. Night night sweetie."

"Night night brother."

He watched her as his sister left the room and went out of sight. The room was enormous to allow enough orifices in there for his thoughts to flow in and out limitlessly. His tiredness hid behind a curious chaos within himself, a chaos he knew not of. Even the cozy bed couldn't help him to sleep and he lay awake trying to close his eyes and only ended up staring at the roof every time. The air about him penetrated fervently through his bosom while love festered in his wounded heart. She was the dream he had always dreamt of and now she was there, flesh and blood, right out of his wonderland sabotaging his peace. The wound, he couldn't decide if it was justifiable to call it so because there was no pain instead a queer pleasure in revising her divine visage again and again in his mind only to fathom that neither had his heart been maimed nor peace destroyed but it was the achievement of true love. He knew it now. Never before had he felt this way about anyone and neither had he ever imagined that he would. Had this been some time earlier back in London he might not have paid much heed to his infatuations, but at this place and time he somehow felt comfortable. An earnest curiosity growing up within him demanded to know what she might be feeling at this moment. Was she going through the same as him? This unrest in his soul would not allow him to stay calm on his bed and he walked towards the window silently staring at the barren sky, brooding over something as he watched the clouds pass by monotonously.

CHAPTER 5

There was always a plethora of pleasantness that lingered in the air when Mohar and Vikram were together. The affectionate aura in the ambience always greeted the two blissful souls with open arms at the usual banks of the Hooghly River. The wet and sticky mud underneath felt good as a peaceful chill penetrated into her body through the flimsy cotton dress that she was wearing. Calcutta's unbearably ordeal summer could be forgotten down here at the cool bank of the Ganga. Vikram stroked his fingers through her sweaty hair admiring the morning beauty by the water, listening to the endearing chirruping of the birds flying around, sometimes interrupted by the careless sounds of the water coming from a distance whenever a boat sailed away quietly.

"Mohar", he said softly as he always spoke and waited for her to respond.

"hmm?", she asked staying laying with her dress sticking to the mud underneath while she fiddled with a weed.

"Why are you so lost today? I'm so not used to seeing you keeping so quiet darling, what's wrong?"

Mohar couldn't stop thinking about the previous night. The handsome man had stolen her peace. She loved wondering about him now and again. Everything around her seemed to be reminding her of the stranger who had preoccupied her brain and about her heart, she was not sure yet.

"Vikram, do you know if someone from London was to arrive at our neighbourhood?"

Her query perplexed the boy as he replied, "none that I know of. Why?"

Mohar tried not to reveal her anxiety about some man she had barely seen the previous night night and tried to be as casual as possible as she replied, "nothing so important, a man took shelter at our place last night and also joined us for dinner because his carriage lost its tailboard somehow. You know how bad a weather it was last night so mother invited him for dinner as well. I have never seen him before."

"And why is it bothering you so much?" said Vikram suspiciously.

"Oh, no, it's nothing. Nothing's bothering me you see, I was just curious, you know." Mohar chuckled as she tried to maintain her tone monotonous and didn't want to sound quite interested. "By the way what were you saying?" she tried to deviate from the topic and she did it quite tactfully.

"Huh", sighed Vikram as he continued speaking after a big sigh. He knew her too well to have missed the anxiousness in her disposition that morning but he preferred not to ask her anything because he knew she would never tell him the truth like always. He knew that she was ultimately going to marry him and may be one day she will fall in love with him. So he felt like ignoring his query and changed the topic very skillfully. "I was wondering if you heard about the party at Lord Curzon's mansion?"

"Hmm—Emma invited me to that party. They are celebrating his birthday and also his son's homecoming."

"Lord Curzon has a son eh?"

"I guess. How do you know about the party?"

"Some of the lawyers at work were discussing about it. Not that I'm interested in attending such parties, was just curious."

"Hey are you jealous?" Mohar sniffed.

"Huh. Why should I be jealous of you because of some party? In fact I'm glad that you will get to enjoy yourself."

Vikram looked quite serious now. He grabbed her shoulders gently and as she sat up straight looking into his eyes he continued, "Mohar, I love watching you whenever you smile. I love to see you happy. I love you Mohar. And it's never enough. Even if I keep saying it all day, because it never seems to explain how much I want to justify those words."

This hysterical situation of emotions didn't seem to affect Mohar as much as it did to Vikram and he could feel a lump in his throat. Mischief sat like an imp on Mohar's shoulders and now it was her turn. She grabbed sum mud silently and slowly pasted on Vikram's face. He didn't dodge back because he knew something like that would be coming. Every time he tried to talk his heart out about his love for her she would use her tricks to avoid the situation as much as possible. A hope that time would teach her to love him had always protected Mohar from any rebut for her unacceptable behavior.

The two of them rose from the ground with mud all over their body and like always ran towards the water hand in hand. They plunged into the water accoutered and Vikram forgot all his complaints with her juvenile laughter.

Mohar reached home all drenched. Mrs. Mukherjee was not at all disappointed with her this time because she knew that her daughter had been with Vikram, the boy she desired to be her son-in-law someday. Mohar ran tip toed to the bathroom to take a shower.

As soon as the water came in contact with her skin she closed her eyes to feel the comfortable cool sensation. But it wasn't at all like always. A sudden gloom seemed to penetrate through her skin and she realized that the shower exhibited its insipidity to the fullest at the moment. An unfathomable bewilderment reminded her of Vikram as his words rang in her ears again and again. Nothing was more expressive of her dilemma than her own meditations then. Why couldn't she feel that selfless love that he felt for her? She did adore him but not enough to compete with his feelings for her. All that never went unaccompanied with pangs of guilt. She clenched her hair hard enough to feel a searing pain that would distract her from the turmoil that vexed her within.

Hardly had she realized that she had been in the bathroom for an hour and a half now. Her eyes burnt because of the waves of water that had been washing them for such a long time and she also thought that somewhere in the midst of her contemplation, tears had escorted her red and swollen eyes. Unwillingly she grabbed the towel and stepped out of the bathroom clumsily.

While she stood staring at herself aimlessly into mirror with a big towel wrapped around her head someone knocked on the door. No sooner had she turned around to answer than her concerned mother trudged in carefully.

"Where has my princess lost into?", she teased her, "is it the realm of love where Vikram has led her to?"

"Stop it ma", she retorted.

"What's wrong Mohar? Why do I see repulsiveness into your eyes darling?"

A thoughtful silence was the daughter's reply. A deep urge to confess her dilemma to her mother contradicted itself within her. She knew her mother wouldn't want to understand her daughter's feelings.

It started worrying Ratna all the more. Curiosity emanated to its fullest extent when Mohar's countenance showed confusion just after she had returned from her meeting with Vikram. A deluge of obnoxious assumptions outran all her abilities to resist her feelings and a helpless series of questionnaire made its way like vomit in front of Mohar.

"Did you have a fight with Vikram or an argument or did he say something bad or—"

Mohar knew that her mother would not stop until and unless she told her what the matter really was.

"Mom, breathe!" she paused, searching for the exact words for the predicament she was facing and then sighed "Vikram loves me a lot. Like really a lot."

"So?", Ratan was too confused to say anything at her girl's inappropriate statement and waited wide-eyed with her eyebrows raised for Mohar to continue. "Is that a problem?"

"Ma I love him too but not the way he does. He's a good friend and also my fiancé but like he says that he feels the pain I feel and I can see the happiness in his eyes when I am happy. I never feel that way for him. I mean I do but not like him. His voice echoes passion every time he says my name, every time he says that he loves me. Are you getting any of this?" she looked expectantly at her mother.

Ratna seemed to buy every bit of what Mohar had just said. "Darling, life's supposed to be that way. Do you know the best cure to this? It is to wait and let time play its part. As time passes you will learn to adjust. Trust me that it is inherent in us since the beginning of mankind." Ratna kissed Mohar on the forehead gently and walked away with solemn steps. Her mother's advice didn't seem to help Mohar at all. Not that she had expected anything more from her mother.

Taking decisions about ones feelings with alacrity is like giving away a five hundred rupee note to a vendor instead of a hundred and before you realize the mistake the man is gone, leaving you rueful for a lifetime. Her thoughts haunted Mohar like wraith so much now that she could feel its presence. She started wondering if she was going mad. It made her nauseous with all the sickening visions that she imagined and averred that if she remained within the frightening four walls of her room anymore she would faint. She ran out of the room and hurtled down the stairs with trembling feet and hair all open, her flimsy white dress swaying away with momentum.

"Where are you going Mohar?!" Ratan yelled aghast as she beheld her daughter running out of the house madly.

"Vikram's place! I'll have lunch with him." Mohar shouted back as if she didn't realize what she was speaking and her only motive was to shut her mother up.

Her mother felt relieved that Mohar had finally decided to talk to him after the strife that was going within her. But what was the urgency? She wondered.

"The whole generation is in a mess. God protect my child." Ratan mumbled to herself.

It was probably one of the hottest afternoons in Kolkata and the obnoxious wind, better known as the Kalbaisakhi had made a pact with the mud to keep swimming around in the air vigorously challenging every species of the existence to dare come out in this weather. Her eyes hurt trying to shun the marauder away but even in this strife with nature Mohar found an amazing peace of mind. All she could think of now was to seek a way out of this chaos and if she had been honest with herself she would find out that her heart wanted this situation to prevail as long as it could, to maintain the distraction. The debilitated girl limped somehow to an old banyan tree by the road for support yet did not hide behind it to fend the gale off. Only a blur of brownish dirt could be seen everywhere.

As she stood panting her dehydrated throat hurt and the taste of dry mud made her feel all the more nauseous.

The pressure was suddenly lowering and the path ahead could now be made out. Mohar was too tired to move she coughed hard to spit out all the dirt that she loathed to carry in her mouth. The gusty wind left its trail and a buzzing sound still lingered around. For a moment she felt that her voice echoed. So she paused to listen to other audible voices scared of what she might have to encounter. She heard the coughing sound again but she could swear it wasn't hers because it sounded masculine.

Weakness was taking its toll on her because of the tramp. Her body demanded water and she felt too sick to move. Squatting by the huge tree she waited for the suspense to unveil itself. A swarthy looking man appeared curiously from behind the trunk. His face, she could say, was familiar but then she wasn't in the plight to recognize him.

The man stooped down to help her get up when she looked up at him and mouthed the word "water" not being able to produce any sound. Her fragile body gave in to the gentleman's sinewy arms that helped her get back on her feet. The two of them limped along until they reached a pond. Mohar was unable to support herself anymore. He sped towards the pond to fetch water for her. First he splashed some water on his face and then picking up a lotus leaf very skillfully turned it in the form of a cone and filled water in it. As she drank back life into herself and sat up only too marveled to see what she yearned to, secretly.

Addie sat staring at her expectantly to make sure that she was alright.

"Are you okay?" he asked. Her face was messy with dirt yet her eyes sparkled and the gentleness in her looks never vanished. But before she could utter anything her head hung backwards as she fell on the mud closing her eyes. Addie rested her head gently on his arms and cleaned her face with his wet hands. As he ran his fingers on her face affectionately the dirt cleaned itself giving way to the bright fairness that he had been so mesmerized to see again. He splashed water on her pale countenance.

"Addison" she spoke as she came back to her senses, coughing. She sat up straight freeing herself from his arms and turning a little pink spoke very softly, "thank you Addie for saving me for the second time." As they sat staring at each other Mohar broke the concentration. "What were you doing out of your house on such a bad day?" she asked not considering her own condition.

"What if I ask you the same question? Why were you braving out jeopardizing your life out there?" he asked her and then continued, "Had I not noticed you limping in the storm what would have become of you? Are you out of you mind?"

She sat quietly not uttering a word sitting with her face drooped down staring at the wet mud. "I was wandering in search of peace." She said blankly.

"Peace?" he asked looking bewildered. "Out in this storm? What were you thinking?"

"That's the best part," said Mohar while she still panted, "you don't get the chance to think anything when you are out in this weather."

Addison was amazed by her remark and as he still stared at her he asked, "What did you say your name was?"

Mohar was fine by now. She loved to see the query on his face. "I have not mentioned my name yet", she said. She seemed to forget all her worries. She was suddenly reminded of his first eye contact with her and was lost in that interesting corner of her house on that night when he had saved her life for the first time. But she was soon distracted by his reply.

"Okay so ma'am may I know your name please?" he smiled.

"No. You may not", she liked to see how much he yearned to know more about him. "I reveal my name only to people who are my friends."

"And am I not your friend ma'am? I have saved your life twice in this week." He looked surprised at her sense of humour and also seemed to be attracted towards her inevitably.

"Well, that does not really make you my friend. They were coincidences. I will let you know of my name the next time we meet, only if we meet again. Only then will I know that we are destined to be friends."

"I don't believe in destiny. I believe in endeavor." He looked a bit serious now. "Our meeting is in our will. We can even meet tonight again only if we wish to."

"No we can't." Mohar told him. "I am not allowed to go out of my house after sunset."

"And what if I assure you that we will meet at sunset?"

"How can you be so sure?"

"Because I am dying to meet you again and I know that the gods will collaborate to arrange our meeting."

"Just because you are dying to see me again doesn't mean that your wish has to come true."

She couldn't look straight in his eyes anymore because deep within her heart she wanted the same too.

"My wish will come true beautiful. You know why? Because it's yours too."

He tried to peep into her concealed feelings forcefully when she allowed him in willingly smiling away and looking on the other side making it all the more evident to him what she felt.

He congratulated himself for having achieved her approval as well for what had been troubling him since the first time he had set eyes on her.

As she looked the other way, to her horror she saw her eldest brother and Vikram advancing towards them from a distance. She stood up immediately dusting the mud off her skirt. She knew the angry look on Sohom's face. As they neared them she started speaking trying to convince him how good Addison had been to her.

"I was stuck in the storm dada when Addie saved my life." she stood dodging her brother resisting him from reaching Addison.

Sohom stopped looking so ferocious now and calmed down on hearing his sister's plea. Instead he extended his arm towards Addison to help him get to his feet as he sat on the mud not realizing when Mohar had stood up suddenly.

In the meantime Vikram pulled Mohar towards him and asked, "What were you doing out in the storm darling? Do you have any idea how worried we all were?

"I-I was going to your house when the storm started." She lied.

"But my house is in the opposite direction Mo."

"Yeah, I uh, I lost directions."

"It's ok let's leave. Come on." Vikram put his hand around Mohar's shoulder affectionately which didn't go amiss to Addie's eyes.

"Thank you Mr. Addison", Sohom was grateful to the stranger for saving their sister's life again.

While the brothers stood talking to the pleasant stranger who had saved their sister for the second time now, Mohar and Vikram turned around quietly and started advancing towards their home. A wave of different feelings struggled to dominate within Mohar as they moved rhythmically hand in hand. She felt pretty suffocated, not being able to express her excitement then on recalling the moment that she had just spent with the foreigner and yet a pang of guilt never left her side when she realized that the man walking with her at that moment should've been the one stirring all the excitement in her, opening to her the different doors of truth that she had willingly shut. Though the physical distance was not much her conscience tried to shout out loud, again and again, showing her the vast invisible chasm between the two souls. As they went farther away Mohar looked back to trace where her new friend was. Her heart twitched to see that he stood motionless still at a distance staring at her, watching her go out of sight.

CHAPTER 6

"Are you okay?", Curzon enquired as soon as his son entered the mansion. "I had asked the servant to tell you about the wind he must have forgotten."

"No he did not, sir, I was well informed about the bad weather, and wondered how bad could it be? Now I know, it's lethal, isn't it."

"Indeed it is, son, and you must not loiter around in the wilderness during such a bad time. However, I suppose you must be in need of a proper bath to wash all that dirt off."

"Oh yes, sir. I will take your leave."

"Let me remind you to hurry up, lest you be late at our meeting in the afternoon. I'll also remind you that we have organized a part tomorrow on the happy occasion of your return, son."

"Wish you a very happy birthday, sir", Addison remembered as he heard of the party. A separation from his father for a long time had created an invisible wall of inhibitions between the father son relationship and Addie found it comfortable to address his reputed father as 'sir' instead of an informal 'papa'.

"Thank you, son." The father and son hugged each other adorably.

Lord Curzon's nervous disposition induced Addie to conclude that something was indubitably wrong about the situation that had engulfed the old man's serenity.

Addie was not the only one who waited on the Viceroy, but he sat with twelve other gentlemen who failed inevitably to overshadow their query about the stranger, underneath their curious brows.

He felt relieved on seeing his father finally, rescuing him from the glares that was getting to his nerves by then.

"Good afternoon gentlemen, please take your seats. I presume we all know that we are gathered here to discuss political matters and better survival strategies. Here, I have some decrees ready to be passed only under the majority of your consents."

To Addie's amazement the men stood up and sat down in a much synchronized manner at the sight of the Viceroy coming in, like they had been practicing it all day long. While he failed to join in he was helplessly some seconds late in following them. Lord Curzon stood waving a fat file in his hand raising it to show the people sitting.

"Each one of you has a similar file resting in front of you. Please go through the reforms that I think, is advisable to be executed. You are allowed to put forth your own perspectives regarding them. The deferments of the reforms are to be executed as soon as they are approved by the committee."

The file was divided into two distinct parts. The first part said "ADMINISTRATIVE" and the next "POLITICAL". He went through the different reforms that his father had set regarding difficult issues and problems. Agricultural, economic, educational and a benevolent famine relief reform too. There were thousands of them.

Addie was still thinking about the girl with whom he had just had a meeting. With every passing imagination her beauty augmented in his heart. There was a big beautiful pink dahlia in the vase which was freshly plucked and still had dew drops on it. It impersonated her subtlety. He beheld her gentle smile as the flower gleamed with the glowing sun falling on it and while he drowned into the depths of his passion something tried to intervene his privacy into his thoughts which annoyed him until he was totally distracted by the

Viceroy who cleared his throat loud enough to alert his son about his next announcement. As he stood upright buttoning his suit he spoke very sternly, "Gentlemen I apologize for intruding in your little business but I have forgotten to introduce to you my son, Addison Curzon, who will be assisting me in my job from now on." He was pointing his arm at Addie when stood up and smiled at the people staring at him.

"Thank you for all your attention gentlemen now please continue with your work."

Addie was not all in the mood to read the official documents then and as he went through the reforms he understood nothing but some random letters that danced about in front of him.

"Son, I don't think you are getting any of that are you?" observed his father. "And so, now, I will be your guide and tell you the situations that my province is facing at this hard time of my career."

"Thank You, Sir." He smiled but was unwilling to hear political stories from his father. As his father spoke invariably, Addie sat looking into his eyes pretending to hear as the Viceroy spoke as softly as possible lest he would disturb the rest of them.

Had it not been for a fat and stout man sitting on the fourth chair from the Viceroy, Addie would have to keep up with his pretension for some time more. He then sat up straight and then leaning forward on the table said, "Sir, I have a doubt regarding the military issues being said here. Sir, don't you think that the three brigades set up needs more of an Indian battalion?"

"Mr. Hopkins, I think that two Indian battalions are enough for the moment. About expansion, we can think of it later. More Indian battalions will outrage them, and with the nationalist spirits brewing up in them, we do not want to defile their trusts, do we?"

Some other men were also encouraged by this objection and they put forth their views too. Addie sat staring at the people talking, listening to them blankly. All of a sudden his father's raised voice caught his attention, though not totally. He heard him shouting something, complaining about the vastness of the empire that he was controlling and also how difficult it was for him to tackle with it.

"Do you even see the huge area Mr. Brown? You—"

While Curzon tried to make his point his son butt in carelessly and while he fiddled with the decanter in front of him, said, "Then divide it."

The noisy hall suddenly fell as silent as a graveyard and also as cold.

"I beg your pardon?"

Everybody in the room stared at him, bewildered.

"If controlling such an enormous empire is the crux of the problem then why don't we consider dividing it in a way that would make it convenient to look after it? We need to look after people's needs. Wouldn't that help? That would only consolidate the Empire's administration and its existence on the whole in this country."

One of the members retorted, "Do you even realize what you are saying young man? Dividing Bengal would mean calling in for a war! The divide and rule policy have been issued many a times before and has proved to be harmful to the empire."

"Who would fight against the government which will work for their own betterment? We will have to talk it out with them. The problem needs a solution, a better strategy Mr. Brawn that is all. Besides who's talking about any policy, it's just going to be a protocol to obstruct the augmenting crisis." Addie saw his father smile at his son's participation.

"We don't talk things out with anybody here Addie. We just IMPOSE them." Curzon spoke finally.

"Sir?" Addie could not decide if he ought to feel intimidated by his own suggestion; if he was being misunderstood.

"Addie, son, you are right a partition—

"division—"

"is needed. But we won't do it. It'll be they themselves who'll do it. So we will have no fear of war or any grudge against the empire," mockery personified his voice alarmingly.

Addie was suddenly worried about his opinion.

"Sir by division I meant division of administrative and political responsibilities."

"That'll be one of them, son. I am very proud of you my boy!" Curzon rose from his seat to embrace his son. Addison couldn't help but feel a happy when he saw his father boast of him though he knew that whatever was happening wasn't for the good. He forgot everything else and affectionately grabbed his father.

"Now that calls for the celebration all the more. Gentlemen I think we should call off the meeting here till the next one."

The men rose from their seats and departed slowly. Addie sat thinking about the whole meeting wondering if anything had gone wrong. He rehearsed the whole thing again as he reclined on the chair comfortably and mumbled to himself, "partition-division. Division-partition."

CHAPTER 7

A pleasant morning in the month of June was not quite of a rarity but today was different. Mohar felt more enthusiastic about going to the temple than ever. The Shiv Mandir situated by the lane which led to the big Maidan would greet Mohar every Monday morning early at 6. Pandit Hirendranath was very fond of the pious young girl, who never missed her regular visits to the temple every week.

"How are you Panditji?" Mohar asked smiling pleasantly as she fidgeted with her dupatta that covered her head.

"Living my life blissfully by God's grace." Pandit ji looked up gesturing towards the sky.

Mohar kept the platter filled with flowers, mainly blue on the ground beside the Shiv Ling and started walking around it while chanting the prayer. The miniature space of a room which was a secluded area from the temple, was built in a corner of the boundary especially for the God of the Gods; Mahadev. Girls would walk bare feet around the temple worshipping Shiva with a belief that by doing so they would get married to a handsome man. This special space for worshipping Shiva was an enclosed cemented area with four openings. It was built in the form of a miniature temple.

With eyes closed and calm temperament Mohar started walking around the God. The first round of her prayer was over but before she could start the next line of prayer, it skipped out of her mind and she could not remember what came next. The reason of her distraction was not known to her. All she did was walk aimlessly with a blank mind around a holy stone staring at the serene, colourful garden outside which went in and out of her sight with the walls obstructing her vision at regular intervals.

She would never have discovered the reason of the disturbance in her mind had she not noticed an intruder to her prayer who could have been punished for the interruption had this been one of those usual times when someone just came in while Mohar sat praying. But today the timing wasn't important anymore because somewhere secretly her prayers had been taken into account. She hid behind one of the walls when she discovered that Addison had been prying on her from behind a hibiscus bush. It suddenly dawned on her that the only disturbance in the ambience for so long had been the movements from behind that tree.

The purpose of the visit was now forgotten and Mohar was now conscious about every step she took from then. She wrapped around the extended part of her saree around her face only to reveal her eyes and walked out of the temple boundaries pretending not to have noticed anyone.

"Wouldn't you take the Prasad Beti?" asked Pandit Hirendranath surprisingly.

"I remembered some work at home I'll come later", said Mohar as she walked as fast as she could with a basket of flowers in her hand.

She stared at the ground as she leapt towards her house as fast as she could. The thumping of his feet grew louder as he came closer from behind her.

"Hey, hey." He called out when they were close enough, "Hey stop."

Mohar was nervous immediately. She stopped suddenly but was afraid to look at him into his eyes. It was too early for anyone to show up on the streets yet she was scared lest it turned out to be one of those days when someone from her neighbourhood wanted to stroll out early in the morning.

Mohar did not look up when Addie spoke, "So we meet again huh."

"But I don't see the sunset." She replied curtly.

"Is that even important anymore?" he smiled. "I just wanted to see you and here you are standing so lively and beautiful like always in front of me. Nothing else matters."

Mohar thanked god that she had hid her face. No one had ever flirted with her before. She took a glance of the surroundings and started walking fast without a word.

It left Addison confused and he followed her, "I guess we can walk then."

"So do you come here every morning?" he asked while he tried to keep pace with her.

"No" was her answer.

"Which God were you worshipping?" he could hear her breath now.

"Lord Shiva."

"Listen why don't you slow down a bit?" he asked politely.

She turned around suddenly before he could prepare himself and they collided into each other. He tried to help her but she dodged him and looking sternly into his eyes she said, "No, you listen to me! I am not allowed to talk to strangers, okay. And let me get this straight to you that we can never be friends. If someone notices me talking to you it'll be really bad. And why have you been following me?"

"Well I'm sorry if I offended you, I didn't mean to. I was not following you. I was out for my regular morning walk and while was crossing that area I saw you worshipping—"

"So that's it. You saw me and then we talked. I'll head home now."

"Hey what are you so scared of?" he looked pretty surprised.

"I know you don't understand but I am not supposed to talk to other men; men I don't know. I love my parents and I wouldn't do anything against their wishes. I respect their decision and I'm happy with it. There shouldn't be distractions now." Mohar mumbled the last few words to herself like she tried to convince her heart about something Addie was utterly confused about.

"What are you talking about? What decision?" he asked bewildered.

"Huh?" Mohar looked blankly at him, "Nothing. I—I—have to go."

Addie was exasperated with her weird behaviour and desperate to talk to her. He could see her expectant eyes. She stood still quietly when he slowly pulled her hood down as he wanted to see her face clearly and they stared at each other. There was no telepathy but some chords definitely matched. She never meant it whenever she called him a stranger because to her heart he was no more a stranger.

"Beautiful" he whispered.

Covering her face again and pulling her hood back on her head she pushed him aside and ran home quickly. Her mother was cooking when Mohar entered the house panting wildly.

"You're home soon." Ratna said smiling. "Mohar why are you panting? Were you running?"

"Yes. There were dogs chasing me." She lied.

"Oh dear, I hope you are alright."

"Don't worry about me so much. I can take care of myself." She said as she ran towards her room.

Ratna stood staring at her daughter's inappropriate conduct and tried to justify it by assuming that it might be one of those bad phases young people go through.

CHAPTER 8

"Why do you look so nervous, Mo?" asked Emma who was trying to read the confusion on Mohar's face.

For the first time in her life she was worried about how she was looking. "H-how do I look, Emma, honestly?"

"Beautiful, like always. Why? Are you expecting someone?"

"Nah—"

"Don't lie so evidently dear, you're already blushing. Who is it? V-i-k—"

Before Emma could finish her word Mohar was already shaking her head ruefully, like she was guilty of something.

"And do I wanna know who the gentleman is?" Emma retorted with exasperation.

"I don't know Emma, I'm suspicious of my own feelings."

A pang of guilt infested her soul and spread like epidemic into her mind and heart. Emma did not know how to react. She rose from her bed and hugged Mohar. The warmth of friendship passed on a pure sense of relief. Mohar grabbed her tightly. She was shaking with fear. She did not know if the worst nightmare was going to happen or may be the best dream was about to come true.

"What are you thinking Mohar? Ask your heart, honey and answer to yourself."

"I dunno Em, I don't think I should do that at all. I am scared that my heart will mislead me."

This grave intercourse was interrupted by Kaka who was calling the girls downstairs because they were leaving for the party. Emma held Mohar's hand tightly and started walking. There was a sudden pause and Mohar bumped into Emma, when she turned around and very affectionately cupped her hands around her friend's cheeks and consoled her, "Let's go for the party Mo, and leave everything to destiny. Just fly with the flow darling and you will see the destination."

Then she held her hand again and reprimanded, "And for god sake Mo! What's wrong with your hands?"

Mohar looked utterly confused and replied, "What? Now you're gonna scold my hands too?!"

"Your hands are cold and sweaty at the same time! Why don't you relax or I'm scared you'll end up falling sick."

Mohar obeyed her friend like a child. And followed her quietly.

An exorbitant party awaited them at the mansion. Mohar sat in a serene corner with Emma quietly and strangely not talking for the first time. She closed her eyes to think of Vikram and how much he loved her. While Vikram played hide and seek behind her eyelids, Addie sat adamantly occupying all the space in her thoughts. Her heart skipped a beat when she thought that she also heard his voice and she shut her eyes harder to concentrate on other things than Addie. To her forced disappointment and furtive relief his voice was not any of her meditations but was as real as her bewilderment.

"Ahem ahem. Hello madam", he said.

"Oh, uh, Hi . . ."

Emma who was looking on the other side jumped up hugging her brother said, "Addie! You're here. Then she turned towards Mohar to introduce her to her brother. "Mo this is my brother Addie and Addie this is my best friend."

Mohar stopped spellbound at his sight. Her wish had come true. "Hello Mr. Addie, nice to meet you." She said.

"Nice to meet you Miss, uh, Mo?" he looked confused. I was wondering if you would like to dance with me."

"Actually I don't—"

Hardly had she finished saying when Emma pushed her towards him playfully and he held her hand and pulled her closer to him. She did not smile, though she wanted to, she just swayed along with him.

"How are you now? You seemed to be quite awestruck in the morning." Mohar asked in a very formal manner.

"I am fine. Thank you. Uh—you look mesmerizing today Mo" he said as he watched her cheeks go red so surprisingly fast as her lips spread into a pretty smile.

"Thank you Addie for the sudden yet flattering compliment."

"You're welcome. But I was curious what Mo stands for. You see I'm not very familiar with Indian names."

I'm afraid you'll have to wait a bit longer." She teased him. It felt like a trivial way but it was an honest quest of her heart to know if the man was in any way interested in her. She was taken to surprise by her own attempts to know someone so badly, because she had never felt this for Vikram ever.

"Is this any kind of a game you're playing assaulting my affectionate query again and again?"

"Don't worry Addie I'll tell you my name very soon."

"And how hard does it have to be?"

"Until I feel satisfied about your endeavors to know me more."

"I think I like the name uh-Mo, till then," he smiled as he spoke skeptically trying to sound funny about the queerness of the name.

As they swayed with the music something very curious caught Addie's attention. In the midst of the soft music that went on he could hear a very sober yet lively tune that Mohar hummed unconsciously to herself with the rhythm. His earnest urge to hear her clearly yet an unwillingness to distract her from the world where she was lost into, put him in a dilemma whether to interrupt her and ask her to sing out loud or not. To his blessed relief the music finally stopped and so did she.

"Hey Mo, I'm going there, down the deserted alley out in the dark alone. This place is too noisy. Would you like to join me?" he came up with a witty suggestion.

"Oh yes of course. I like the silent darkness." They had something in common already.

Emma looked at him worriedly while they strolled away happily not bothering about anything else.

The street was silent already, though it was not too late. The sky showcased a violent tinge of a romantic freshness which was accompanied by a very attractive fragrance of flowers around.

Addie finally took a deep breath and broke the unnatural yet enchanting silence, "I cannot stop wondering what that thing you were humming so beautifully in between the dance was?"

"You heard that?" she felt happy secretly.

"Of course I did. How could I miss such a beautiful melody? The music seemed to be collaborating with you. Amazing tune, it was. Mo, could you sing it for me now, out loud?"

"Well thank you Addie, but I'm afraid if I sing it for you now I don't think you will enjoy it as you did in there."

"And what makes you say that?"

"That song is one of Tagore's songs it is in Bengali you won't get a word."

"Who's Tagore?"

"See?"

"Okay I was just joking. I know who he is. And about the Bengali part, I think you will translate it for me, won't you?"

"Yes I will but are you sure?"

"Please, I insist."

"Okay."

Along the way with a rhythmic breeze blowing around Mohar was again lost into her melodious world and every word she uttered unveiled its clarity so swiftly and gently like she meant every bit of it.

> *"Jaagorone jaay bibhabori—*
> *Aankhi hotey ghum nilo hori—ke nilo hori? Mori mori!*
> *Jaagorone jaay bibhabori—"*

As she sang the whole song, Mohar could only feel for none but Addie from the very core of her heart.

Just like Mohar had said earlier, Addie did not understand a word that she sang, but her voice tickled his heart and the sweetness of the song had automatically created music that he could hear with the passing rhythmic air. He didn't want to her to stop. His eyes were fixed on her as she walked two steps ahead of him sometimes hopping and then swirling around like a pretty doll. Then she stopped silent, and bowed down giggling. Addie stood clapping, beaming at her.

"Why did you stop?"

"Did you get any of it?"

"Of course I didn't but I loved it Mo, trust me. You sing like some fairy tale princesses."

Her gloomy countenance told him that the song wasn't a very happy one.

"Why don't you tell me the meaning of the song princess?"

"In my sleepless nights, a stranger keeps me awake, a stranger who stays unknown to me, whom I yearn to find in my solitude yet his flute echoes in my heart. The serenity of the lonely night conveys secret messages to my heart that is filled with pain and my eyes brimmed with tears, yet I see his curious shadow trembling now and then."

"Who is it, Mo?"

They stood facing each other in the deserted street when Mohar got her answer but she was too scared to accept it to herself, answering the foreigner was out of question.

"Oh Addie, that's just a song", she lied unconvincingly.

They walked side by side rhythmically looking around here and there trying to avoid each other's eye contacts lest they would get caught. The leaves sang their beautiful musing witnessing the two souls who were falling secretly in love with each other.

She felt an awkwardness in her heart, some invisible strings held back what she was feeling while she tried hard to fight them back.

Addie realized that he was leaning on her physically and may be a part of him even emotionally as they sat on a nearby bench built by the pavement usually for hawkers. Unconsciously his deep admiration for her, intensified with every silently passing breeze from between them and gradually led him to stare at her. A strong twitch in his heart told him that he was falling for her, though he was very convincingly skeptical about any further progress of this relationship. Rather he was scared, that his feelings might be irrevocable and since he was unaware of her side of the story, a fear of a heart break crept into him. He wanted her to know about it. What he was not sure of was if she would take him seriously because it was too soon for anything like this. He tried to stop himself but words made their way out like vomit and he spoke helplessly.

"Mo every time I see you my heart beats way faster than it can keep a count of itself. I don't know why but I can't stop thinking about you from the day I saw you. Or maybe I do. Well I do know why. It is because; because I have fallen in love with you. Your presence makes me believe in happiness. Your existence defines the purity of my feelings. I want you to know that I have finally heard my heart's musings and I want you to hear yours and tell me what they are saying."

She had turned pink, Mohar thanked the darkness for keeping it concealed; but apparently it was too late. Addie had already smelled a rat. Between his dilemma and fear a miniscule particle of hope cropped up wherein lay his heart. In the midst of the dark silence of the street the girl's words had given him courage to extend his hand very carefully, and while she showed no sign of denial, telepathy worked by which they knew that they were in love with each other. But before they could move any closer to each other Shohom, one of Mohar's elder brothers stood calling out for her. Hardly had she heard his footsteps when she stood up erect leaving him behind.

"Dadabhai" she said nervously.

"It's quite late. Let's go home." He said looking disappointed. "I met your friend Emma in the hall where I was expecting to see you, but then she told me that you had left long back."

"Uh, Dabhai we were just talking how cold it is back there in London." She tried to distract him from staring at Addison but he would not stop.

She attempted in vain to convince his brother that they were "just" sitting there casually for a chat. Her brother's unusual silence rang the bell of ultimate fear into her ears. She obeyed him without another word. Before leaving she turned back half way to see Addie once from the corner of her eye and then started walking swiftly with her brother.

"Look kid, you are at an age when red and pink flowers, love poems and all that stuff seem to be life, but trust me those are just fantasies, and are very alluring. I don't have a problem with that either. But if suddenly a monster gets into it as an imposter of love and tries to hurt my little princess, I'll have to kill him. Like the, uh—(he thought for a second and then realized) there are no brothers in fairy tales, are there?" A very concerned yet very polite brother spoke to his little sister and tried to be funny unsuccessfully to make sure that he didn't scare her off.

"You're worrying just for nothing dabhai—"

"Ugh darling I am not ready to listen to any of your airy-fairy explanations, okay. Now let's go home like nothing happened and from tomorrow you don't meet him ever again.

"But—"

"EVER. AGAIN."

She knew it would be useless to back chat so she kept mum and walked along with her brother sadly, pretending to agree with him.

CHAPTER 9

Mohar did not know what time it had been but she knew for sure that it was quite late because the only source of sound around her was the random barking of the dogs occasionally. She knew that the only person in the family who would even get close to understand the mayhem going on within her was her mother and she could not wait for the morning to show up so that she would confide her little secret into her mother. No sooner did she decide to tell her mother about it than she changed her mind. She rolled on her bed from one side to the other and then again talked to herself like she was trying to explain someone that she was not wrong. She started singing to herself, smiling and shying away as the lyrics demanded her to do. Then for a moment she went blank. Nothing going on in her mind but she was not at peace. She closed her eyes and tried to sleep. Her mind tickled her heart and her body felt playful as she smiled at her own misery. An undaunted courage spoke from somewhere within her encouraging her to gift herself the fulfillment of her wishes while practicality knocked to prove its semblance in this whole hullaballoo of emotions and pulled her back from even wondering about something like that.

Suddenly she recalled what had happened to her own aunt Sarba when she dared to marry the man of her own choice. People called her shameless and also went to the extent of questioning her character. Now she was compelled to live in the outskirts of the village and where no one could see her lest she would turn out to be a bad influence on the upcoming generations. Mohar adored her aunt and had also visited her secretly a few times with Vikram.

A very strange intuition told her that someone was knocking on the door. It was only then that she realized that she might have woken up someone with her song. She waited to make sure if someone had actually knocked on the door. There was another knock. But it didn't seem to come from the door. Instead, to her horror it was coming from the balcony door! A chill went through her. She was scared as she tip toed towards the door. Before she could reach there was another knock. She reached for the door and with trembling fingers opened the door. But there was no one at the balcony. Apparently someone had been standing down in the garden and throwing stones at the door. The lights could not be switched on lest people would know. So she took the lantern with her. Her heart pounded as she beheld the most beloved sight that she had been longing for from the core of her heart. Addison stood gesturing something to her in the dark but she could not understand a thing that he said.

Suddenly she came up with an idea and gestured him to wait. He saw her disappear in the dark while he waited. Every second out in the dark seemed to Addie like an hour, but before long, to his relief Mohar showed up with the lantern again.

She had a bottle in her hand which had a string fastened around it at its neck. The bottle was lowered to him with help of the string. Addie took the bottle and found a letter inside it. As he opened the cork and overturned the bottled on his hand the letter found its way out. It was fastened around a pen, so that he could reply back. Mohar extended the lantern so that he could read the contents of her letter and also write back a proper reply. All she could see was his shadowy silhouette and assume that he could only be Addie, because her heart said so.

"Are you out of your mind? My brothers will kill you if they found out", he read out murmuring to himself and smiled. Then he rested the piece of paper on his lap and scribbled something. When he was done he rolled the paper around the pen just like she had done and gave it a pull so that she would take it back.

"I couldn't stand the ignorance of not knowing your name anymore. It was not allowing me even a wink of a sleep." Her feelings strengthened itself as her heart made sure of his. She wrote her name beneath his line, "Mohar Mukherjee" and lowered the bottle again.

As she extended the light to help him see the name tears made her eyes warm, when she saw him kiss her name on the paper. She smiled like she had never smiled before. It is true that until today she was suspicious about the phrase butterflies in the stomach. Something tickled her as she read the reply, "I have never heard a prettier name before."

There was a space of about a line or two and again written, "When can I expect to see you again?"

She wondered what to say for a moment and then as he saw her silhouette move she fidgeted with something and then again with the paper lowered the bottle to him.

He found a gold earring in it and the letter read, "Hope to see you soon."

As she pulled the bottle back she read in the letter, "Take the light near your face Mohar."

She did as she was told as she saw his dark figure hop some steps backwards his head tilted in a position so that he could admire her beauty, like he loathed to turn back and then turning back he just disappeared into the bushes of her garden.

She stood there motionless for a long time scared of the future and feeling guilty about something that was not wrong. A sudden noise indicating motion inside the house told her that she should back to her bed now. She was too excited to feel anything. Vikram didn't even seem to hover anywhere near her romantic thoughts.

CHAPTER 10

Days had just become hours of patient waiting for Mohar, since nights were the best moments of her life that she spent now-a-days. Vikram would visit her every evening like the routine. Mohar hated the fact that she couldn't share her secrets with her best friend rather pretend like she was normal.

He made her feel guilty sometimes when he said, "Mohar you've changed a lot. You look distracted. What's going on in your mind? Just tell me already or kill me." He would joke.

She would try to explain but he got none of it for obvious reasons. "Look, Vikram" she started speaking enunciating every word aloud like she wanted him to pick up hints about her love life, "I am going through a tough time now. I'm fighting with myself everyday to get rid of all this happening," she paused to breath and then continued, "but I can't, I want to stop because it's gone too far now. I just want you to be there for me as the best friend as you always were to me."

Vikram had understood all of it. He finally saw his hopes diminish totally. It was then that he realized that her heart belonged to someone else now. Yet he decided to pretend that he failed to fathom what she was talking about and gave her cold blank looks and said, "Mohar, what's wrong?"

Mohar just smiled away and said calmly, "Oh I think it's just a bad phase and it'll go. I mean, I had a small fight with my mother and I'm figure things out."

Vikram wanted to give up what he wasn't aware was that love was also a synonym of hope and his love wouldn't allow him to stop hoping that someday she would be all his.

Mohar's brothers were home from there a while later and they walked into the room where they sat chatting. Shohom patted in Vikram's back and joked, "Hey pal, now stop flattering my sister and come out of the house, we are getting late for the game. They say we have a new player."

Mohar knew it immediately who the new player was and jumped up saying, "Okay then let's go."

Shohom turned around and said, "Whoa girl, you better ask mother before saying that. It's already getting dark outside."

"Dabhai, Vikram, you guys will talk to mother about it, won't you?" she looked like a little child while she begged them to tie the bell around the cat's neck.

"See! I hate you when you do that!" said Shohom as he grumbled his way to the kitchen.

They could hear Ratna's voice echo like a banshee throughout the house as her brother convinced her to take his sister along with him to watch the game.

Mohar's heart skipped a beat every time Addie stole a glance at her. He looked as handsome as a Greek God with his tall and muscular physic as he ran for runs. How badly she wished she could call out Addie's name and cheer for him but the little sister of five hefty brothers was not allowed to cheer for anyone or comment on anything or even laugh out loudly or make any gestures to anyone to attract attention. She was so engrossed in admiring the love of her life that she had not realized when the other half of the bench was occupied by Emma.

"So what's going on?" she asked.

Mohar moved with a start, "God! You scared me."

"Why? Were you stealing something? A glance may be?" Emma smiled winking at her friend.

"Stop acting smart Em, and tell me what the matter is?"

"Me?" she asked, "You should be telling me stories now."

"What stories?" Mohar tried to give her a confused look.

"Oh come on Mo, Addie has been staying out of bed since a couple of nights now, he looks more distracted than he has ever been all these days and—"

Before she could finish her sentence the boys shouted out something. Addie had barely got away from Vikram's ball which had apparently been aimed at his face.

The girls were still looking at Addie when Emma finished her statement "and Vikram is trying to kill my brother so please tell me what the matter is."

"Okay!" she gave in "we are in love. Your brother and I, we are in love with each other. There you go, I said it."

Emma stared at her friend, "Did I just hear you saying that you're in big trouble or was it something else you are trying to say?"

"Look I know it's going to be a really difficult situation to get through with it but we'll figure things out, okay. I don't know how but we will." Mohar explained.

"Mo, you don't know what you're talking about. You've gone bonkers!"

"Yes I know. I'm crazily in love right now and I have never felt like this before. But I respect my parents way too much to dishonor their trust you know."

That was something Emma didn't like. She could never figure out how falling in love with someone had anything to do with respecting one's parents. "Hey you are in love. How is that disrespecting your elders?" she said.

"You don't get it, Em." She tried to explain.

"Well then educate me." Emma insisted.

"Look they trusted me to the extent of being so liberal with me all my life and now when it's my turn to play my part I can't back off like a coward. I have to face it, okay."

Emma looked blank as she retorted, "Mo they did whatever they had to because that was their duty why do you have you have to pay back anything?"

"No Emma. They could've got me married to Vikram by now—"

"But then they'll do that today or tomorrow, so what's the point in waiting."

Mohar didn't know what to say. She was too confused so she kept quiet.

The two girls sat talking while Vikram carried on with his attempts to hurt Addie physically till the game was over.

While they were leaving Addie came running to talk to his sister and she immediately knew what had attracted him towards her. "Let's go Em." He smiled at Mohar while her cheeks went pink.

"ahem ahem" Emma cleared her throat, "let's go."

Vikram was also there before they could leave "Let's go Mohar" he said looking sternly at Addie.

CHAPTER 11

"Shall we tell Sir Addison about it?", asked Mark suspiciously.

"What do you mean?", said the Viceroy.

"The other day at the meeting, he seemed to be opposing every time you talked about the partition, sir and moreover do you think he's going to let us execute it when he comes to know the truth and with all the lovey-dovey time he spends with that Indian girl."

Lord Curzon recalled the meeting and realized that Mark wasn't wrong.

"I am impressed Mark, with your observance. You are right about the boy. But by what you are suggesting, do you want to say that we shouldn't call any meeting regarding this matter, rather call the concerned people secretly and confide into them the plan?"

"I am trying to say exactly the same, Sir."

The two of them spent some time pondering over their decision. Neither of them talked to the other while they sat looking out of the window wondering to themselves if they were correct about the plan.

"Sir." Mark interrupted the serenity. "I think we should send Sir Addison away on a holiday."

"Send him away? Where to?"

"Anywhere to run on some errands. We could tell him that your friend Sir John Lestrange, who stays in London wants to talk about this partition and that we have decided to send Sir Addison for the job since was keen on maintaining a protocol."

"You think that's goin' to work?" said Lord Curzon since he cared more for his son's feelings.

"Yes, of course. Why not?"

"What shall we tell him when he returns?"

"The truth of course. Isn't it obvious that a country with so many different creeds and castes and religions might as well have a bit of vendetta sometimes? After all they are all human beings. Their thoughts are bound to clash at some point. Don't worry please, nothing will go wrong."

The two of them smiled rather wryly at each other.

"Bring the two glasses from over there, Mark, let's drink to our decision."

Mark brought the bottle from the rack and poured some wine for them smiling helplessly to himself and patting himself secretly for his wit.

"Cheers!" drank the two conspirators.

CHAPTER 12

Hardly had the Mukherjee men left for the court when the mansion greeted Addie with open arms. One of the servants opened the door, as he stood fidgeting with his hair and suit and kept peeking into the glass on the door to make sure he was looking as charming as always. A big smile on the man's face welcomed him as he entered into the pleasant house of the Mukherjee's. Ratna appeared from somewhere behind the hall to attend the guest. She did not look very happy on encountering with Addie that morning; neither did she showcase any disappointment by her cordial behavior.

"Oh. Addison, Good morning," she smiled.

"Good morning Mrs. Mukherjee."

"What brings you here this early, it better be something very urgent." she tried to be sarcastic.

"Oh, uh, yes. I mean, Emma, found this earring on the floor the other night after the party. She wanted me to give it back to Mohar." He tried to explain for his odd visit.

Mrs. Mukherjee looked suspiciously and started questioning him.

"How do you know Emma?" was her first question.

"Uh, actually she happens to be my sister." Addison smiled again.

"Why didn't she come to return the ring?" Ratna was still not smiling.

"My sister f-f-fell ill this morning." He lied.

Though Mrs. Mukherjee was not satisfied with his answer because his stammering had not gone amiss her notice, yet she realized that she was being rude to her guest and it was not right, so she ignored her anxiety and gave in to his stories.

"Oh I see. Das babu", she called out to the servant, "take the sahib upstairs where bibiji is singing."

"Come Sahib."

Addie was still skeptical about Mrs. Mukherjee's approval about their meeting. None but Ratna was the only person from the family to be aware of their friendship. Her disposition, however, had never been very affectionate towards him; nor had she ever misbehaved. Mohar's witty explanation about her relationship with Addie rendered it impossible for her mother to disprove it; also with passing time Addie's excellent sense of social propriety had won a bit of her adoration by now.

As he stood near the wide door of the spacious room, Mohar sat inside; cross legged on an antique couch with a long stringed instrument which she played while she sang beautifully. All this went in and out of his sight with the stark white drape that floated into the air from one side to the other with the blowing breeze.

As she started winding up, Addie entered into the room with his hands into his pockets. He loved the way she smiled at him affectionately every time they met.

"Hi, when did you come?"

"Just a while ago . . ."

"Ugh, you were standing by the door again? Why?"

"I love to hear you sing, I didn't want to interrupt you dear."

"But with all this less time that I get to see you, you shouldn't do that."

"Oh my poor girl, you look so pretty when you make that face."

"Now don't do that because it won't help."

"Prettier." He joked.

"Oh Addie stop it." She smiled.

Her rosy lips spread on her face and the tinge of pink on her cheeks was all the more visible on her fair skin; all of that gave birth to a strong urge in him to cuddle her. His soft fingers coloured her cheeks while they ran down her face to her neck as he sat embracing her with his arms around her. The cool breeze comforted her as she felt the warmth of his body. But before long the usual fear was back and she unfastened his arms though she hated to do so and moved away from him.

"Mother keeps loitering around in the house. I don't want to stop seeing you Addie."

"It's okay. I understand. Hey will you sing that song for me; the one that you were just singing?"

"No."

"Wow that was pretty quick for an answer."

"I meant not that one, but I do have a song in mind. The song that I had kept in my heart all these days for the one person for whom my heart will sing and not me."

"And you think that person is me?"

"Yes I am pretty sure of it. I have never sung this song for any one before and neither will I sing this one for anyone other than you after today."

Addie sat curiously on the extended window sill while she sat on the couch singing her heart out.

Amaro porano jaha chai

Tumi tai, tumi tai go

Amaro porano jaha chai

Toma chhara aar a jogote

Mor keho nai kichu nai go

Amaro porano jaha chai

Her voice echoed through the mansion, melody expressed itself to the fullest with the intense love that accompanied the ambience. She meant every bit of the song that exposed vehemently all the veiled, unspoken feelings and exploded within her like a volcano where the song oozed out in the form of hot lava, filled with passion.

Her eyes were moist when she finished singing and Addie came closer to wipe her tears off. While his warm fingers ran through her eyes clearing away the agony that had made its way through her eyes, she spoke monotonously; her voice still shaking hysterically.

"You are the one that my heart yearns for

You are the love of my life

Nothing but u can make me happy

Without you I am nothing; I have nothing and I can think of nothing

You're my world and without you in it I do not exist."

"I cannot sing my love, but if you listen carefully enough that's what my heart sings too. Just like yours." He kissed on her eyes as he said so.

"The strong invisible walls between us won't let me hear them, Addie."

"Why don't we forget about them for once?"

"I can't. I can't be so selfish. The woman downstairs trusted me enough to have left us up here, considering our privacy and not telling a word to anyone in the house for all these days; the man who thinks I'm his pride will die of a heart attack the moment he comes to know that the only regret in his life was his only daughter whom he had given all that love and freedom that she needed, going against the society that wanted to suppress her; the five brothers will stop trusting themselves to have opposed their mother all the while she kept warning them; and the person next door will lose all his wishes, all of them, the ones he kept very safely in his heart in the hope that one day they will come true, he will be shattered into bits and pieces."

"They are all you are worrying about? Where in the name of love am I, in that list, Mohar?"

"You are not there in that list because you are the opposition. You are the one that makes me all weak and lures me to be selfish and very mean to all those people. When I see you I feel like nothing else is more important and that I can betray the world for you."

"Bloody hell Mohar, sounds like I've turned you into a monster! Where's the meek and gentle little girl I had saved from getting crushed that night? You don't have to abandon anybody for me love. You think I don't understand any of this?"

"I don't know. Look I'm sorry okay. I didn't mean any of that, I'm just too bewildered to say anything right now. Help me out of this Addie. Rescue me from this pain."

She broke down into his arms weeping to herself.

"Hey, hey, don't cry. We will figure this out soon. We can't give up on this just like that okay. Just have some faith in me, please."

"You are the only hope I have, Addie. I trust you."

"Now do I want to see a smile on that face?"

Mohar forced a smile languorously wiping off the tears from her cheeks.

Ratna stood languidly at the door clearing her throat purposely to distract the two of them.

"Mr. Curzon, it's time for Mohar's father to come home for lunch. I think it's best if you leave now."

"Oh yes Mrs. Mukherjee I was about to leave."

Unlike the other days Ratna kept standing there adamantly not giving them their time to say a proper good bye. The two of them felt uncomfortable to talk in front of the mother so Addie just mumbled a "good-bye" and walked away quickly.

"You heard all of it, didn't you mother?"

"Yes I did."

"Look you don't have to worry about anything okay."

The mother felt her heart give a twitch at her daughter's condition. She sat on the couch holding her daughter close to her bosom as the woebegone lady spoke with a heavy heart.

"I never realized when my little princess had grown up so much. You know kid, when we are at an age like yours there are some things that seem to be permanent and very attractive. It might also convince us to believe our life has no meaning without that thing. Darling everything is not at all so easy. Do you think that your relationship will survive when you start staying together? This boy is very nice. But he doesn't belong here. If by any chance you two get together how do you think you will spend your life with him? He doesn't even understand what you sing for him. He is not accustomed to our culture, neither will he ever be."

"Ma, I love him and so does he. When we start staying together we will learn to adjust because we will love staying together."

"All that vanishes when responsibilities start showing up suddenly. Moreover the moment you're gone with him people around here will kick us out of the neighborhood. They would say that we are a bad influence on them. Already your father has always opposed the world and given your freedom just like the boys. You don't want to prove him wrong and all those bad neighbors out there right, do you? You know that it will shatter him, right?"

The girl's pallid face moistened her mother's blouse as she was wreathed with utter gloom. Sometimes the heat of a moment forces some decisions upon us and that's when we tend to take the worst ones in our life. That moment whatever had possessed her she knew not of but she could bet that it had forced her to promise some really wrong things to her mother. The woman distracted Mohar from the intense love for the British and convinced her emotionally.

"I won't marry him ma, I won't let daddy down by any means. I'll marry Vikram, ma I promise."

A sense of victory tickled the witty woman. She took the little girl downstairs for lunch congratulating herself secretly.

CHAPTER 13

Mohar was too confused about ending things with Addie. She couldn't have fallen so deeply in love with a man whom she had hardly known for a month. Was that even possible? It was dark and probably midnight. Addie should have been there by now. Before she could rack her brains any further the usual rock hit her door. She was not at all excited like the other days today instead she was scared. Just like her normal schedule she took the lantern and the paper in the bottle and strolled out at the balcony. She glanced furtively at him looking all stolid while he smiled adorably at her sight. As the bottle reached the ground he opened it hastily to read its content.

"You didn't return my earing" it read.

He looked up at her. The darkness hid her countenance but her mere presence made his heart at peace. He scribbled straining his eyes in the dark, with the very little sources of light from here and there and a bit from the lantern held far above. She pulled the bottle up when he gave the string a pull indicating that he was done writing.

"That will never go back to you, in fact its pair will come to me with you." She read.

Tears rolled down her cheeks and she didn't want to stop them today. As she sat down leaning on the railing he could see her hold the note near her heart and shake vigorously as she cried. Shouting out to her would be calling danger for both of them and there was nothing around through he could climb up to her. There was nothing he could do but stand their helplessly and see her break down in agony.

He waited for her to stand back and reply. It was killing him to see her in the condition he would never have wanted her to be especially when the reason for her misery appeared to be him. To his relief she stood up but before he could smile she turned her back on him and walked inside. He also thought that he heard the door close behind her.

As she waited by the door the thumping of his steps faded as he scurried through the garden to his way out the mansion gates. The rigours of this would always keep its trail on her, she knew it for sure. Addison will hate her from this day onwards. Little had she known that once you fall in love with someone you stop feeling anything else for that person, but love and no matter however nonsensical their activities might be you will always try to reason that out because trust comes gratis with the love and separation ceases to exist even in the wildest nightmares.

CHAPTER 14

Lord Curzon sat smoking pipes all night. He was too tensed to get any sleep all night. He stood staring out of the window with his pipe in his hand. There were birds chirruping outside which indicated the arrival of dawn. A very thin streak of a blend of maroon and golden light sieved in through the sky when suddenly something very unusual caught his attention. A shadowy figure was jogging towards his mansion. It was only later that he realized that it was his own son. He was immediately suspicious about his son's whereabouts at this time of the day.

"My son seems to be spending a lot of time with the Indians of late it seems," said Lord Curzon. "Is he still meeting the girl, Mark? Do you know anything about it?"

"Sir Addison has indeed been seen around with the girl a couple of times now, sir. But it has just been a month and it is still not too late. If we wait any further lest Sir Addison gets emotionally attached to this country and its people . . ."

"Don't you worry about that Mark." The Viceroy interrupted him.

"Whatever we do it has to be done soon I suggest," said Mark.

"What'd you say we'd tell him Mark?"

"The errand, sir, I hope you remember? Your friend Sir John Lestrange wanted to discuss about the partition, so we can send Sir Addison for that, can't we?"

"Oh yes, I do remember. But he needs to be convinced properly. After all he's my son."

Addison confirmed himself the first thing when he woke was that the previous night had not been a nightmare. He wanted to talk to her. He looked at the clock it was 12noon! Why hadn't anyone woken him up? Now the only time he could see Mohar was at night. He trudged towards the bathroom unwillingly.

Addie was called the moment he was done freshening up. Little had he known what his father would come up with at that moment.

"Hello Sir." He smiled

"Hello son. How have you been? You seem to be very busy nowadays."

"I'm very well thank you." His father's unusually polite tone did not go amiss his notice. "I like loitering around in the wilderness. It's a pleasant place down here. Don't have much to do, do I? Moreover I have started taking a liking towards the people here."

So Mark was right about Addison's emotional attachment towards the country.

"Well then I have the exact thing for you. I want you to run on an errand for me to London."

"That sounds great. So what's the work and when do I have to leave?"

"My friend and governor of London would discuss some political matters with you and since he is a busy man we could fix the meeting for the day after tomorrow. I think that you will have to leave by nightfall. We have arranged your transportation."

"But Sir—"

"I know dear that we are sending you on a short notice but I want you to know that the news was sudden for us too. We are really sorry we are rushing you this way. Moreover since it's been a few days since you've arrived I think it is high time you start becoming more politically involved."

"Oh no, it's fine Sir. After all it is work and that is why I am here. Moreover London is like my home. I'm glad you chose me for this work."

"Well then I hope you need to go to your room and pack things up real quick."

"Yes I'd better be off then."

Addie walked lousily to his room burdened with a load of thoughts. He wished he had enough time to talk to Mohar before leaving. He wouldn't be able to see her for at least a week now. All his stuff was packed when he finally realized how much he was going to miss her. Her voice rang in his ears as he sat into the carriage while it carried him away. He couldn't help imagining the day he had arrived here and there in that mansion, it had all a month ago and now it seemed like he'd known her for ages. She had become a part of his life. These incredible moments with her had been the best time of his life. He was reliving all the romantic moments spent with Mohar while the carriage sped through the silent street. He had secret plans of may be talk to Mohar's family about their marriage when he returned.

CHAPTER 15

Three days had passed and Mohar had not yet heard from Addie. She was already starting to worry.

"I knew he was fooling around. I knew some day he would just go back to London and forget about you. May be he'll return with his new bride this time." That was all Ratna had to say about him.

Though Mohar didn't believe in any of this, yet the thought of losing him would scare her off sometimes. Vikram would still be visiting her every evening. That was the only moment that she didn't feel lonely and left out.

"Why do you look so pale these days, sweetheart? Where has all the fun gone from your life?" he asked one evening.

"It must be something else, you are misjudging dear," she forced a smile trying to conceal her worries.

"Has that ever happened before, Mohar?"

She kept mum thinking about something that would distract him. Then she came up with, "I haven't heard from your mother lately. How is she doing?"

"Had this been one of the moments by the river, Mo I would have replied to your silly question. But now let's face it. I have no more hopes about this relationship. You think I have no idea what has been going on these days? I was under the wrong impression that you at least consider me to be your best friend. Since when have we known each other Mo? Since eternity, since we were born and I have loved you ever since. Why wouldn't you tell me?"

She was all aghast. She didn't know what to say, so she just tried to convince him that whatever he was thinking was not at all true.

"Vikram it's not at all what you are thinking."

Vikram had always been considerate with her, but today he knew that he had lost her. He was on the brink of breaking down when he succumbed to his rage that kept him balanced on his feet.

"Then what the hell is it?!" he yelled at her for the first time in sixteen years.

She was shaking with fear. This was the highest point of toleration for Vikram and Mohar could fathom that very well. A big lump in her throat prevented her from uttering a word.

Vikram continued shouting, "What do you think you have been doing then silly girl? Were you just fooling around with that foreigner?! Every bloody time you thought you fooled me with your bloody tactics of distracting me whenever I wanted to talk serious stuff with you, you had been fooling yourself! I used to forget about it, because I had hopes that someday you will realize how much I have always loved you! I thought you need some more time. I was trying my best to keep up with your nonsense and then bam! That son of a bitch appears from nowhere and takes you away from me!" he was all red with a searing pain in his heart when it dawned on him what he was doing. Tears made way inevitably and now he had calmed down. He sat on the floor leaning against the wall as he witnessed a blurry image of Mohar standing quietly at one corner. He seemed to be coming back to normal and then he continued, "You could have told me, sweetheart. Why would you sneak him in behind my back? At least I thought that you considered me to be a good friend and now you've even stopped being a friend to me honey."

"I was afraid and confused and all torn apart", she cried out loud. Her voice trembled as she spoke. Vikram I love you, you are my best friend but trust me I've always taken you for granted and your things have always been mine but I never considered you as a husband, like, you know and then Addie came along and I felt all berserk and yet wanted to avert all the consequences and then I didn't know what to do with dabhai reacting so weird and . . ."

"Hey hey hey, relax." Vikram got up to his feet and advancing towards Mohar sat on thew couch, just next to her. He grabbed her right shoulder gently and apologized, "Honey I'm sorry. Please don't cry."

She broke down crying aloud into his arms. "I am sorry Vikram. I didn't want to break your heart dear" she held on him tight and he wrapped his arms around her to console her. The two them were helpless yet sympathized each other's condition.

"Mohar", Ratna called from downstairs, "come down for dinner kid and Vikram, sonny, your servant, Hari has come along to fetch you. He says that your mother wants you to run on some errand."

Vikram wiped her tears gently and kissed her on the forehead, then helping her stand up said, "Mo, no matter whatever happens I'll always be there for you. Don't worry he'll be back soon and I don't want to see those tears anymore. Now come on let's go."

Hardly had Vikram stepped out of the house when Mohar joined her mother to give her a hand in laying the table. Mohar was wipiing the wet china plates when her mother retorted, "have you heard what people are talking about you madam? It has become difficult for your father to even sit among friends in the neighbourhood. People are asking questions. Vikram is such an innocent little boy; he ignored all that and came here to visit you. At least he didn't run away!"

"Addie didn't run away ma! He'll return soon."

"Now you listen to me!" Ratna yelled at the top of her voice. "You have already done enough okay. Now you will do what I say. Your father and I will go to Vikram's place tomorrow to talk about your marriage and you silly girl, you don't have a say in this okay!"

Shohom was reading in his study when he heard his mother shout insanely. He came running to see what was going on. Mohar was quite relieved at the sight of her brother. Hardly had she known that this was one of those rare situations when her brother wouldn't take her side. She looked at him expectantly when he turned to his mother and said, "what is it ma?"

"Do something about this girl Shoho, or she'll invite her own doom someday."

"Don't you worry about it ma. Vikram is a nice guy, he'll bring out the best in her; I'm sure. I just hope that everything goes on well tomorrow." This was the first time when her brother gave Mohar a cold look of which she had never known of.

She was aghast. She knew that no one was kidding and that she had no escape this time. Everyone was quiet at dinner. The elusiveness and mire of the moment left her meditations all maimed and her mind was blank and so was her countenance. She strolled towards her room with an utterly nervous disposition. While she rehearsed the nightmare that had just come true some moments ago at the dinner table, it suddenly dawned on her that a bigger one yet awaited her. What would happen tomorrow? Will they ask her to marry Vikram before even Addie returned? When would he return? What if he never returned? But why would he do that? She sat on her bed leaning on the window and stared outside.

This was where I first saw him. I wish I could see him again now.

She was reminded of her mother's story which she had told her so many times since last year. "I didn't even know how your father looked when I got married. I wasn't happy about it either but you see my parents knew what was good for me. It was difficult at first but then we bargained with the situation and see how happy I am." That was all she had to say about her marriage.

I don't want to make adjustments like mom. I want to be happy and not bargain with my happiness. What do I do? How do I stop this? Addie where are you?

The darkness outside seemed to be permanent that would never go away from her life, where the only silver lining was Addie, who was nowhere to be seen now.

CHAPTER 16

"So it's been long since Sir Addison left sir. When will we execute the plan?"

"I think tomorrow is the day. What do you say Mark?"

"Consider it done sir."

The two gentlemen had been awake at this time of the night to discuss their secret strategy about their new divide and rule policy; that is to break the unity of the Indians on the basis of religion. The Indians on the other hand didn't actually realize what the Government was planning and was very likely to fall prey to their sly measures.

CHAPTER 17

Mohar beheld light making its way through the black canvas and wished her life too had faced such illuminations. Some innocent birds were chirruping outside when the canvas was being painted maroon and violet at same time. The cry of the crickets was now fading with the morning freshness and new life. The new morning seemed unknown and utterly unusual to her. This was definitely not like the other days. The new sunrise would bring new changes in her life today. Hardly had she known what fate had in store for her.

When she woke up her head was heavy. She didn't remember when she'd dozed off amidst her worries. There wasn't a word to be heard from anyone in the house. It was 11 already.

They must have left for Vikram's place, she thought.

She was obviously not allowed there because only elders were allowed to be present at places where they met to decide their children's lives. The street outside had also fallen silent at this time of the day when it ought to be the most active. She wondered if she was still in a trance, looking carefully out of the window.

Is the whole world mourning for my doom?

There was crashing sound downstairs which confirmed the presence of another living thing in the house. She strode through her way to find out the source of the noise. She found that their old and haggard servant had dropped a couple of chinaware while cleaning them.

Ratna was a newly wedded bride when Shambhunath Kaka came along with Mr. Mukherjee to help the couple with their new life. He was quite young then. Mohar also adored him a lot just like a grandchild would love a grandparent and it was the same with Kaka too.

"Kaka, have they gone already?"

"Oh yes baby they'd left quite early. It's time for them to be back soon." The conspicuous lines of tension on her countenance and awkward disposition didn't seem to have missed kaka's notice. "Mohar, kid, are you alright, child? You look sick."

"Ah yes, I'm okay." She lied.

She felt that her eyes had swollen and her shoulders and arms were paining because of the awkward position she had passed out on her bed she realized.

A proper shower may help me get back to normal.

Dragging her feet unwillingly she forced herself into the bathroom. The cold water calmed down her anxiety while she stood still to feel its perfection. When she stepped out of the bathroom the clock caught her attention. Suddenly she was aware of the deadly silence and awestricken by the time. It was already 3 in the afternoon and no sign of a creature outside or in her house. What was taking them so long? She grabbed a saree randomly from the shelf wrapped it round her hastily and ran downstairs all vexed calling out to Shambhunath.

"Kaka! Kaka!"

She found him sitting on the last stair looking all tensed.

"Oh baby I know you must be getting worried about them."

"Yeah kaka. Why don't you go and check what's taking them so long?"

"Yes I would have but I can't leave you alone in the house. Moreover I don't see a person outside. I don't feel very pleasant about it."

"Ugh kaka I'm fine trust me. I'll lock the doors properly and don't you worry about me just get me word from them.

"Fine I'll go if you insist so much but if master scolds me I'll tell him that you forced me to go."

"Yes. Okay. Now just scoot!"

The servant left quickly, with an umbrella to avoid the heat.

The empty and silent house suddenly haunted her and she was afraid of its stillness for the first time in her life. An hour had passed since kaka left and there was no sign of them returning neither any sign of livelihood out in the streets. Mohar paced up and down the hall nervously. She could feel her heart palpitating. The sudden news of her marriage with Vikram, Addie's disappearance, nothing mattered right now. Squatting on the ground she buried her face into her haunches.

After a while; she didn't know how long she'd been sitting on the ground; a faint noise distracted her attention. It seemed to be advancing nearer as some men roaring with anger became more and more audible. Mohar stood up scared of what might just happen and started running upstairs. The marauders banged on the heavy iron gates outside. Mohar locked herself into the bathroom. She heard stones being thrown into the house which shattered the glass windows. Deep within her she hoped that Addie would suddenly appear from somewhere and save her. The bathroom seemed to be the safest place to hide at that moment. She regretted the fact that she forgot to grab a knife or some other means of protection from the kitchen downstairs.

The cold floor corresponded with the feeling in her heart. A chill went through her. Something terrible was coming. Murmurs of her sobs echoed in the bathroom as she sat shivering with fear and anxiety. Why were people after her life? Where was her family? She had no idea how she ought to react in a situation like this.

The uncompromisingly cruel cries of terror seemed to subside when Mohar realized that the ambience was not unlike a graveyard. Thousand different thoughts raised her mind. She couldn't help thinking that something bad must've happened to her family. She gathered courage and got up to her feet. The demons banging on the door had either left thinking that the house was empty or maybe they were trying to break in from the terrace. While she tip toed down the stairs she prayed to god that her family should be alright. Apparently someone did barge in from behind her nearly giving her a heart attack. The mere hint of someone's presence around her scared her to the fullest as she leapt forward running hard with strides towards the kitchen to grab a knife for her protection. She sensed the stalker run after her when she thought she heard a familiar voice.

"Mohar! Mohar, baby, it's me! It's me Vikram."

Had there been some normal passerby at the moment he was likely to mistake Mohar's cheerfulness at his sight to be irrevocably passionate love, but it was actually relief and anxiety. The broken glass pieces scattered on the floor didn't seem to affect her much as Mohar ran into her best friend's arms crying the fear out of her.

But this time he was in a hurry. He put his hand on her mouth so that her voice was not audible and pulled her into the space under the staircase as they sat still in the dark. Before Mohar could question anything she became aware of footsteps coming down from the terrace.

Some men could be heard talking. Their vague voices made it impossible for the two of them to make out what their intentions were. But their movement got louder as they advanced closer. "I don't think the lawyer's at home pal!" the roughness in the man's voice scared her off. Suddenly to her horror she could see his shadow on the wall and she thought she saw the shadow of a knife in the man's hand. She held Vikram tightly and let out a gasp of fear and a short inevitable cry made its way out of nowhere. The marauders who had turned around to leave suddenly ran downstairs.

Vikram pulled Mohar by her arm and dragged her towards the kitchen but before they could go far one of the attackers threw a knife at Vikram and while he barely made out with it, the weapon was sharp enough to scrape off a bit of his skin from his left arm with the edge of the thing. Mohar shrieked out terrified. Vikram pushed her aside and picking up the knife that had fallen on the ground and aimed it back at him. It struck him on his leg but his companion was untouched and he advanced towards Mohar. She couldn't run fast as her feet were bleeding because of the broken glass pieces. The heavy glass fruit container was all that she could think at the moment and she threw it at the man. It hit him on his head and he collapsed to the ground bleeding from his forehead. Vikram tried to see if Mohar was alright when the other man came running with a knife towards them. This was it. They felt that this was the end. The cry of vengeance echoed in the mansion and before the beast could harm them Vikram kicked him on his belly and he fell to the ground he snatched his knife and stabbed him right through his throat. Mohar fell to the ground witnessing the most horrible sight in her life. Vikram ran towards her as he grabbed her with his bloody hands.

Mohar looked too much in a state of shock to say anything. Vikram shook her hard and yelled at her.

"Mohar say something!"

To his relief she finally spoke, "What do we do next?"

"Get some of your necessary stuff from upstairs, we'll have to leave this place as soon as possible."

She stood awestruck, "Where are my parents and where will we go? Who were they? Are there more of them out there?"

Vikram had never before this, given such stern orders, "Just do as I say and I'll explain everything. We are going to your aunt Sarba's place at Nabardeep." He was still panting, fighting to grab some air.

For the first time in her life Mohar didn't question any further. She trusted him. A few clothes, a mirror, her tooth brush and a comb was all she could remember to take at that moment. She knew her parents would be safe and might as well meet her at his aunt's place.

He looked down on the floor suddenly only to notice some red pieces of broken glass which led him to see the red footprints that had gone upstairs. His eyes followed the footprints and stopped at Mohar who was already done packing and limped down with the bag that she assiduously hung on her right shoulder. He leapt up to her and grabbed the bag only to sit down by her feet to witness the unnoticed wound.

"We need first aid here!"

"No Vikram I'm okay. Let's leave." She wanted to meet her parents, besides she was too frightened to feel any pain.

Any casual friend wouldn't have noticed the difference in his attitude if it hadn't been for Mohar, when Vikram seemed to be fine with Mohar's disapproval about getting a first aid while escaping seemed to be his priority over Mohar, which could as well be explained, went against his rule. He stood up erect grabbed her bag again and holding her by the hand sped towards the road. They took a short cut towards the station and boarded the train to Mayapur. Mohar was aghast. She knew something really horrible might have occurred. She tried asking him what the matter really was but he would not answer. He just said, "Don't ask questions now."

They reached Mayapur and then hired a boat to go to the other side of the river where lay the small village of Nabardeep.

CHAPTER 18

Had she been informed beforehand about her niece's arrival Sarba wouldn't have been worried so much at their sight from a distance that she dropped the broom and stood motionless till Mohar and Vikram reached her house.

"Mohar, Vikram. How come you people didn't give me any message before coming?"

Mohar hugged her and said, "Haven't my parents come yet?"

Aunt Sarba looked bewildered. "Your parents? Why would they come here?" Her expectant glance shifted to Vikram who hung his face staring at the floor.

Mohar turned around and like a child begged of him to speak. "Vikram, please say something. Where are our parents? Where are my brothers?"

Vikram broke down crying, as he fell on the ground whispering to him. "They're dead. They're dead." He sat crying helplessly.

Mohar stared blankly at him. She sat down by his side and holding his face towards her she asked, "What did you just say? I don't think I heard it right?"

"Yes you did. You heard me right. Our parents are dead, Mohar." He circled his arms around her waist and grabbing her with all his agony cried out aloud like a little boy. Her wounded feet that stung till then had become numb and she wished she could also cry out all her anguish like him, but the sudden news had obliterated all her abilities to even react. The sky seemed to be falling towards her and the floor shook underneath when she fainted, on the ground.

Sarba wiped her tears immediately helping Vikram to bring the girl into the house. She sprinkled water on her face but without any results. Mohar lay as numb as ever. Vikram lowered down his face to kiss her forehead and holding her tight wept incessantly.

He had fallen asleep by the bed when the woman came in with some food for the kids. She didn't want to disturb them so she left the food covered on the table beside the bed.

"Vikram" she woke him up. "Come on kid let's get your wound cleaned before it gets worse." Vikram got up against will and obeyed his aunt.

It was dark outside when Mohar came to her senses. She didn't know what time it was. How long had she been out? She stirred a bit only to feel something soft in her hands which felt like fur. She leaned to look sideways. Vikram was sitting on the ground by the bed resting his head on his folded right elbow beside her. She stroked through his hair gently.

He woke up with a start. His head was paining and elbow was numb because of the awkwardness of his position and his wounded arm stung real bad. Mohar wanted him to sit beside her on the bed, but she couldn't speak a word. Like always he knew what she wanted. Getting up on his feet he sat by her caressing her hair and without any warning started speaking in a blank tone.

"Early in the morning today, when Pandit ji was about to enter the Krishna Temple, he found three beheaded cows lying at the doorstep. He knew it wasn't a coincidence. He gathered the villagers and people assumed that this was done by the Muslims. Some lads spread the rumor that the Muslims were trying to insult our religion and they started barging into houses and slaughtered three Muslim priests as revenge. It didn't take long for the news to spread along and the other parties to come out of their houses with weapons to avenge their loss. Before anybody could realize a massive riot had broken out. When our parents sat discussing matters at my place a bunch of Muslim men broke into our house with swords and choppers. The boys and I were in my room having our little talk. By the time we came out to see what the matter was they had already done their job. Shohom was injured trying to save Shibu. We fought back killing two of the lads while three of them escaped. Your brothers took away Shibu to the hospital when they sent me to bring you here. They asked me not to tell you anything at first because we knew had I told you all this earlier you would never agree to come here with me. They say it was one of the sly tricks the British are trying to play but who will tell the fools about it."

Tears rolled down his cheeks continuously as he sat narrating the painful experience. Her face too was all moist with tears

"And kaka?" she whispered.

"He never showed up."

After a long moment of silence he said, "All I'm left with is you."

A faint light was visible in the horizon. It was then that they realized that it was dawn. He noticed that Mohar's eyes had swollen and she had quite visible dark circles by now. She had not spoken a word properly since she heard the news. He ran his fingers gently on her cheeks when she fell asleep again. Before he could realize he passed out beside her on the bed.

It was twilight when Vikram woke up. He walked towards the door. His eyes burnt as he rubbed them carelessly not feeling any bit of the pain.

"I tried waking you up but you were fast asleep and wouldn't even stir." Her aunt complained, as the widow sat lighting a lamp. "Look son", she said wiping off sweat from her forehead with her saree, "you have to be strong now, at least for the girl. What's gone will never come back but what's still left with you, hold on tight to that."

He didn't have the strength to listen to her now. He trudged towards the bathroom and slammed the door behind him. He filled buckets with cold water and emptied them one after another over himself trying to cool his agony.

CHAPTER 19

It had been a whole day and a half since when the kids didn't have any food nor did they crave for any. Mohar was down with high fever by now and aunt Sarba was getting worried. She reprimanded Vikram for acting insane though she herself was depressed because of the loss of her only sister. Yet she stayed strong enough and very diligently fulfilled the responsibility of being the aunt of the kid. She used some local medications and forced Mohar to have some food which would help her heal sooner. Her wounded feet were bandaged very carefully. Aunt Sarba had never had children and she adored Vikram like her own son and Mohar was like her daughter. She brought some warm water. Straps of cloths were dipped in it. Her eyes felt the warmth as she put the straps on them. A sudden relief spread through her swollen eyes.

After the two kids have been looked after properly Aunt Sarba left them alone for some time.

"Mohar, we have nothing left back there. Some of the necessary stuff that we've left behind, have to be taken. I don't think I'll be able to stay in that city anymore. Two days are about to end and neither Shibu nor Shohom has contacted us."

Mohar finally spoke for the first time in two days. "Why did you have to save me, Vikram?"

"This is not the time to ask silly questions. Once we go back, I'll see if Addie has returned or not. If he hasn't I'll take you away with me to our ancestral home in Burdhman. We will stay there till I establish myself somewhere in the city again. If Addie has returned and he comes searching for you, then you're free to marry him. But I won't leave until I see you settled down properly."

"Seriously? You want to talk about it now?" Mohar was angry.

Vikram seemed to be practical now. "Yes I do. Because we need to talk sense now. Do you think that this riot will end so soon? This was just a mere start. People won't let us survive there peacefully. As soon as we get there we'll have to pack and leave. We can hardly stay there for a day or two. I won't leave you to die there. I'll take you with me."

He took the lamp and rose from the bed walking towards the door. "It's quite late, go off to sleep. Gotta get up early tomorrow."

She lay awake in the dark crying helplessly to herself. The Mukherjee Mansion called her back every now then. Her childhood, Emma, and her brothers, everything seemed to happen all over again in her mind. She hopped about in her veranda dancing on her first Rabindra Sangeet. Her mother's voice echoed into her ears, the song written by Tagore,

"foole foole dhole dhole bohe kiba mridu boye"

Then her father would come home from office and ask her to do her little jig. All the day's exhaustion seemed to vanish with his daughter's smile. Her brothers had always adored her like their most precious possession. She remembered her fifth birthday when her brothers had gifted her, a room full of dolls and her favorite teddy bears and how they supported her whenever her mother scolded her. She knew no worries. Had it not been for some juvenile falls she wouldn't have experienced what crying was like.

Even when there were sad moments, Vikram always came to her rescue. Time passed, she grew up and then Addie came into her life. She fell in love with him. Now she needed him and the only one who was there for her was Vikram like always. She was reminded of her song that she sung to Addie which seemed to be the best moments of her life and then the last song. Would she never meet him again? Was that all supposed to be a forgotten dream? Her mother's last words rang into her ears. She had wanted Mohar to get married to Vikram. May be she was right. She called out to her mother aloud

"Mom, come back to me please. I will do whatever you want me to. Just come back. Talk to me."

She fell from her bed and cried harder, yelling with all her anguish this time. All her suppressed grief burst like lava from a volcano as she sat weeping monotonously on the ground.

Vikram lay silently on his bed when he heard his love wailing in the middle of the night. He hopped out of his bed, lit the lamp and hurried towards her room. He found her lying on the ground, trembling as she sobbed. His finger loosened suddenly at the sight and awestricken as he was, the lamp fell off his hands and rolled away. He grabbed her immediately forcing her to calm down. Nothing seemed to sooth her at that moment. She held him tight and sobbed louder.

The incipience of a feeling of responsibility rendered him calm and patient enough to help the girl stop crying as she passed out into his arms. Initially he felt that he could leave the girl alone but she was too emaciated with grief to be left unattended, he decided later.

Vikram was right. Mohar had a disturbed sleep. She would wake up screaming at times and then fall asleep crying to herself. Travelling was not advisable at this state so he decided to postpone their departure for a day.

CHAPTER 20

Aunt Sarba wiped her tears as the two young kids set off for their journey towards uncertainty. Mohar and Vikram were too tired to even talk. They were sick with the grief of their loss. Mohar felt guilty for hiding things from her family. She wanted to tell them everything now. But it was too late.

After a long journey they reached. The door was broken, just as they had left it. In all probability it had greeted more visitors or may be killers. Something was unusual. The house had been cleaned. Someone was inside the house! As she shouted, "Dadabhai!!" like a wish had been granted to her by a fairy god mother Kali showed up from inside. "Chhorda!" Mohar ran towards her brother. Her eyes were swollen already and now they were burning again as tears rolled down her cheeks. Shohom and Shibu showed up from behind too. They grabbed her sister as soon as they saw her.

"We'd never thought we'd see you again. Thank you Vikram." They walked towards Vikram. He looked very sick. His eyes had gone into a hollow. "Come on in you two."

While Shohom sat next to his sister caressing her hair and soothing her, Shibu and Kali took Vikram into the house.

"How's Shibu da now?" Mohar asked.

"He's recovering, but the damage that has gone deep into our hearts will never heal."

Mohar lay into her brother's warm arms when he told her what they were planning to do next.

"Mohar, we don't have much time in our hands. Whatever we are planning we got to do it fast. This is war of the religions and these people won't stop now. And our houses, Vikram's and ours; with hideous memories like these in them we will never be able to settle in them anymore. So we have decided to sell them when things calm down. For now Shibu, Kali and I are planning go somewhere out of Bengal to set our own law firm and join hands with the freedom fighters all over the country; enough of fooling around for us now."

Mohar heard silently while she wondered how blissful her life had been and that this situation was something she had never imagined in her life.

"I hope you understand that we are really worried about you", her brother continued.

She nodded.

"So we want you to marry Vikram by tomorrow and leave for his ancestral place after that. At least we'll be at peace that our little sister is happy. Look we do not want to force things . . ."

"I'm okay with that dadabhai", she interrupted. She was too tired to say anything. Moreover she remembered her promise she had made to her mother. At a time like this when she was missing her the most all she wanted was to obey what she had promised to her dead parent who seemed to be watching her from somewhere. Somehow it felt that it would make her mother happy for the last time.

"They say that the riot is just another strategy of the British to break the country's unity," said her brother.

"It's good, though whatever you are planning to do." Mohar realized. "I just hope that I'll get to see you guys often after that."

"Of course you'll get to see us. We will come down to meet our little sister every now and then", he consoled her.

"Come on now let's go upstairs. The boys must be waiting for us."

Her brothers and Vikram suddenly stop doing whatever they were doing and stared at both of them as soon as they reached the door. "She has agreed" said Shohom happily when they sighed with relief. Vikram didn't look overwhelmed though, Shohom patted on his shoulder, he assumed that Vikram might have been upset about the riot yet."

Mohar was making dinner with whatever was there in the fridge when Vikram sneaked in.

"Mohar, I wanna talk to you. Meet me at the terrace after everyone's asleep."

She didn't speak a word when he turned around and left."

Everybody was quiet at the dinner table. They were all still traumatized with the horror that had just passed. They finished the food as fast as possible and left for their beds.

When Mohar crept out of her bed silently she could still hear her brothers murmur about their future plans. It was too dark for them to notice that their sister was silently out of her bed. When she reached there was no one on the terrace. Addison's house was so prominent from the terrace that she thought she could see him moving on his terrace. Past thoughts tortured her mind when Vikram arrived.

"I'm sorry to have kept you waiting, your brothers wouldn't stop talking." He apologized.

"It's ok." I heard them while I was coming upstairs.

"So, we're getting married tomorrow huh." He said blankly.

Mohar was surprised with the coldness in his voice. "Why do you seem so unhappy about it?"

"Because you are not happy."

"But no one's forcing me into this. I agreed to marry you."

"Mohar I'll go looking for Addison to their house tomorrow. I don't want to feel like I took advantage of our situation."

"You don't really have to do that. My brothers—"

"Well I will convince your brothers if I find him and he agrees to come with me."

Mohar couldn't stop her tears. He held her tight when she asked fumbling for words, "Why 'er yer doin' this?"

"Because I love you", came the honest reply.

He helped her pull herself up and said, "Let's go now. Tomorrow's a big day."

Mohar stopped him by his hand and whispered softly, "I love you Vikram. You are indeed the best friend I will ever have. You are an angel."

Vikram had turned and said immediately, "Now off to bed before I change my mind."

They went down silently to their beds.

CHAPTER 21

When Addison entered the city he couldn't recognize it anymore. There were burnt houses, sabotaged gardens, blood splatter here there on the walls garbage everywhere and not one soul to be seen around. When he started walking an old, withered man came limping towards him crying. He had seen the man somewhere. Mohar's place he recognized.

"Kaka!", he said aghast. "What happened to you?"

The man was swearing at his sight that left him all bewildered.

"Kaka," he shook him, "What's wrong and where are the Mukherjee's?"

The old man could barely speak, "All dead. Your father! You! And your foreigner friends! Haven't you had enough? Why did you come back? What more do you want?" the man spat in hatred and walked away.

Addison couldn't imagine anything and was too awestruck to react. He found his father's carriage waiting for him. He climbed on it, "take me home as fast as you can!"

The streets were barren and at places there were dead animals. A foul smell lingered around as he reached home.

He ran into the house and yelled "Father! Father!"

Lord Curzon came out with a pipe in his hand as if nothing had happened hugged his son and said, "Welcome my son so how did the meeting go?"

"You tricked me!" he shouted pointing at his father. "Mr. Lestrange told me that they were planning on an admininstrative division and we were planning for that all these days while you slaughtered people over here like butchers!"

"You must listen to me first, son," he said calmly. "You are new to this country you might not know this but these religious strife are quite common here. It is their local vendetta son."

"Liar!" he yelled. "You started it. You kindled the fight didn't you? Didn't you?! That's the policy! DIVIDE AND RULE, isn't it?!"

"Well you suggested it. Remember son?" he said his father.

Addison was quiet for the moment. He felt guilty. It suddenly dawned on him that he was the reason for all this that had happened. His advice had been taken in an utterly wrong manner.

While the men tried to settle score Emma came running and hugged her brother tightly. He felt her shaking terribly. He grabbed her sister and with his heart pounding he asked her, "Is she dead, Emma? Is Mohar dead?"

He was scared to look at Emma into her eyes when to his relief she shook her head.

She stammered as she sobbed and tried to speak at the same time, "Her parents had been killed when Vikram took her away. Vikram's parents are dead as well. Her brothers, she and Vikram have returned the day before yesterday. Father wouldn't let me go see her anymore. Now that everyone knows the reason of the riot she wouldn't even like to see my face. Addie, bring her home before she goes away."

"It's too late now." Addison sat on the ground.

"No it's not. She needs to know that you were not at fault at all. Promise me Addie that you'll let her know."

Addison wanted the same, though he didn't hope that she would forgive him for what had happened. "I will visit her after sometime, I promise. Okay?"

CHAPTER 22

Vikram was getting ready to leave for Addison's house when someone knocked on the door. Kaali opened the door. Addison's mere sight riled the Mukherjee brothers when they came down on Addison. They thumped him with a few fists when Vikram came running to save him.

"Stop it guys! Let him speak."

Vikram helped him stand up on his feet when he panted, "Can I meet Mohar please?"

Shibu came towards him furiously when Vikram calmed him down again.

"Talk to us if you have to our sister doesn't want to see your face!" then he turned towards Vikram and said "If he takes any step forward I promise you he won't get out alive."

Addison said, "look, guys I don't want to fight you. I just want to talk to Mohar. But since you don't want me to I will not go against your wish but would you please give her this letter and let her decide if she wants to see me or not? Please?"

Vikram convinced the brothers. They stood there like sentinels when he took the letter to Mohar.

Mohar stood listening to all of that in her room upstairs. Vikram stood with the letter when she opened it. It read:

Dear Mohar,

I don't know how to start and what to say. I know that you have been through a lot while I was away. I hope you trust me. I hope you don't hate me like the others. It is true that the riot was a part of our plan but trust me love I knew nothing about it. I had suggested an ethical division and these people started slaughtering human beings. I was not aware of their intentions at all. Mohar I can't stop loving you. It is on you to decide now, whether you want to come with me or not. You just say a yes and no power in this world will be able to stop me from taking you away. My heart lies with you and your earing still waits for its pair.

Love
Addison

Mohar finished reading the letter and started folding it hastily. "What happened? Shall I call him upstairs?" asked Vikram.

"If I see him now I'll see my parents' blood in his hands and their cries on his face, Vikram. Just ask him to leave."

Her grief for her loss overpowered her love for Addison and the fact that he was somewhere related to her parents' murder would never allow her to live peacefully with that man, ever.

She had cried way too much to feel anything anymore. The separation impaled her heart but the moment wasn't right. She was not in the state to feel anything. That afternoon she was married to Vikram at the temple.

They left the place by evening. Mohar and Vikram sat in the carriage leaving behind the most memorable times of their lives. Mohar could hear her cries, her songs, Vikrams tantrums, her mom's advice, her father calling out to her, her brothers' voices, and Addie's musings, all asking her to stay back, while she shut her ears to them and cuddled into Vikrams arms who held her tight trying to fight his emotions. He shunned away all the voices calling out to him. His parents, childhood, love, vendetta, all of them shut away and bade good bye to the land which gave him everything and took 'em back from him as well.

SIX YEARS LATER

"Mohar get up my love, here's breakfast. You need to have food on time." Vikram woke her up caressing her hair. The sunrays disturbed her as he helped her sit upright on the bed. He put some pillows behind her back and after kissing her forehead he bent down to kiss her belly which had conspicuously bulged out to reveal her pregnancy. Her lips spread into a satisfying smile. It reminded her of the horrid past from where they had moved on. They had never imagined life could be this normal ever again.

"I'll leave for the court now ok, if you need anything just ask Maloti to get it for you. Bye hone."

"Bye Vikram." She smiled adorably. He had been the reason she could bring heart back to one piece after it had been impaled again and again. She ran her hand gently over her belly and could bring heart back to one piece after it had been impaled again and again. She ran her hand gently over her belly and congratulated herself. She was missing her family. A brisk walk around the house would help all the time but today she wanted to see them. For the first time in 6years she pulled out the trunk from under her bed. Everything came back as she opened it. Pictures of her parents, her brothers, memories flying out alive. The wounds returned back, felt so fresh, when she her eyes fell on a piece of paper. Perhaps it hid a few more under it. She pulled out the chits. The one's they would use to communicate from the balcony at night; she and Addison, the love of her life. There it lay; the final letter written by him to her. She read it and reread it again. A sudden yet unwelcomed quest cropped up from nowhere; a quest to know if anything would have changed had she waited. Would she have forgiven him by now? Was he really not aware of anything at all? Had he been blameworthy he wouldn't have come to her giving an explanation.

She was suddenly distracted from her thoughts and she found her eyes moist. It was high time she got rid of these stuff. She had no right to ruin Vikram's trust this way because she loved him too.

"Maloti" she called out to the maid.

She came running not seeing her mistress in her room. "Why are you sitting on the ground Mam, why didn't you call me?"

Mohar stood up ignoring her and ordered her, "pick up this trunk I want to go to the beach."

"But ma' am—"

"Call the driver with the car."

Maloti obeyed her mistress who had never been this restless before.

In no time the car arrived. Mohar didn't speak a word on the way. Maloti didn't want to disturb her either.

The car came to a stop when they reached. She stepped out silently embracing the soft breeze blowing. The cold water washed her feet when she closed her eyes to feel the serenity. It pained her heart instead to finally get rid of the past. She asked her servant to empty the trunk into the sea. She watched them go away. The blood stained photographs, her old clothes, broken toys dried up flowers and drops of tears which were getting lost with the waves. As she saw her past going away with the waves she secretly opened her fist and peaked at a letter that she had decided not to give up at the last moment; the last letter that Addie had ever written to her.

"Leave the trunk here", she said softly and walked towards the car.

There lay the empty trunk, in the middle of nowhere . . . the one that once carried memories of a lifetime.